She was unable to take another step. A hauntingly familiar voice reached her ears.

He sat by the bed, his head bent close to Nick's. He was talking baseball and he had the boy's full attention.

His shoulders were slightly broader than she remembered, his chest wider, but no gray marred the thick, dark hair. The hand that lay lightly on the bed rails was the same, too—lean, strong.

Kent Berger hadn't changed. And oh, God, she'd never realized how much Nick looked like him. The shape of his face, the way he cocked his head to listen, even the half smile. She'd never let herself notice. Would *he?*

Please, no, she begged. She must have made a sound of supplication, because he looked up.

And for the first time in eleven years, Mallory stared into the eyes of the man who could save her son's life—his real father.

Dear Reader,

Only he can save her son, the son he doesn't know is his.

When her son, Nick, is diagnosed with leukemia, Mallory Brenner places him in the care of Dr. Kent Berger, the man who fathered him. Now she must face the most difficult decision of her life—to tell Kent the truth or keep her secret. And as Hanukkah, the holiday that celebrates a miracle, approaches, she hopes for her own miracle: life for her child.

Eerily, soon after I began this book, my husband, Ralph, was diagnosed with acute myelogenous leukemia, the same illness Nick has. I completed this story as Ralph waged a courageous battle for his life, and I promised him I'd finish it on time. I dedicate this book to his memory and I plan to donate part of my royalties to the Leukemia-Lymphoma Society as a memorial to him.

Lorna Michaels

A CANDLE
FOR NICK

LORNA MICHAELS

Silhouette®

SPECIAL EDITION®

Published by Silhouette Books

America's Publisher of Contemporary Romance

 SILHOUETTE BOOKS

ISBN-13: 978-0-373-24794-3
ISBN-10:   0-373-24794-X

A CANDLE FOR NICK

Copyright © 2006 by Thelma Zirkelbach

Books by Lorna Michaels

Silhouette Special Edition

A Candle for Nick #1794

Silhouette Intimate Moments

The Truth About Elyssa #1124
Stranger in Her Arms #1349

LORNA MICHAELS

When she was four years old, Lorna Michaels decided she would become a writer. But it wasn't until she read her first romance that she found her niche. Since then she's been a winner of numerous writing contests, a double Romance Writer's of America Golden Heart finalist and a nominee for *Romantic Times BOOKclub* Love and Laughter Award. A self-confessed romantic, she loves to spend her evenings writing happily-ever-after stories. During the day she's a speech pathologist with a busy private practice. Though she leads a double life, both her careers focus on communication. As a speech pathologist, she works with children who have communication disorders. In her writing, she deals with men and women who overcome barriers to communication as they forge lasting relationships.

Besides working and writing, Lorna enjoys reading everything from cereal boxes to Greek tragedy, interacting with the two cats who own her, watching basketball games and traveling. In 2002 she realized her dream of visiting Antarctica. Nothing thrills her more than hearing from readers. You can e-mail her at lmichaels@zyzy.com.

For my husband.

Chapter One

"Hey, Mom, Rick Howard hit another home run. I bet he breaks his record."

Mallory Brenner stepped into the family room, where her ten-year-old son sprawled on the couch, remote in hand, watching a New York Yankees baseball game. She ruffled his chestnut-brown hair. "Hey, son, I bet Nicholas Brenner breaks *his* record for the most home runs in Little League."

He grinned, showing a mouthful of braces. "Bet you're right."

Then he scowled as she leaned over him, thermometer in hand, and ordered, "Open."

He did. As his hero rounded third though, he mumbled, "If we lived in New York instead of Valerosa, Texas, we could see Rick Howard play."

Mallory removed the thermometer, set it again and stuck it back in Nick's mouth. "Haven't you noticed? You *are* seeing him play, right here in our living room, through the modern miracle of television." Nick muttered disgustedly and she held up a hand. "Now zip your lip and watch the game, or I'll have to start over again."

Nick turned his attention to the TV and kept quiet. The thermometer beeped and Mallory checked the reading. "Normal. Second day in a row."

"Cool. Think Dr. Sanders will let me play ball now? It's been a year."

"A *month*," she corrected, then added, "I'm sure he will, as soon as he gets the results of your blood test."

The last week of April, Nick had come down with the flu.

Usually quick to shake off any illness, he hadn't been able to recover from this one. Their family doctor had been at a loss to explain the lingering fever and weakness and had ordered a complete blood count.

"When's he gonna find out?" A whiny note appeared in Nick's voice. "I'm *tired* of laying around here."

"We should hear today. Tomorrow at the latest." Seeing Nick's lower lip inching toward a pout, she quickly suggested, "How about some ice cream? I picked up a quart of Baseball Nut."

Nick pushed a pillow onto the floor. "No."

Mallory sighed and prayed for patience. "Come on, Nick, it's your favorite. And you hardly ate any lunch."

He glared at her. "I'm not hungry."

"Why don't I set up the chess set and we'll have a game before I go to work?

"It's your day off."

"Lauri's kids are in a swim meet this afternoon. I promised I'd come in around four and relieve her." Her partner, Lauri Gold, had put in plenty of extra time at Buds and Blossoms, their florist shop, since Nick had been ill. Mallory was glad to do a favor in return. She'd already made arrangements to drop Nick off at her parents' for the couple of hours she'd be gone. She patted Nick's shoulder. "How about that game?"

"You're not very good," Nick grumbled. "I beat you the last four times we played."

Patience, she told herself. "Hey, nobody beats Mallory Brenner five times in a row."

Deciding to interpret his grimace as a smile, Mallory got the chess set. They were setting up the pieces when the phone rang. "Be right back." She went into the kitchen and picked up the receiver.

"Mrs. Brenner, this is Kelly from Dr. Sanders's office. He'd like you to stop by to discuss Nicholas's blood test."

Stop by? To discuss the results of a routine blood test? Alarm bells went off in Mallory's mind, and she grasped the edge of the kitchen counter. "I have to be at work soon. Can't we do this on the phone?"

"I, um, don't know. He asked me to have you come into the office. He said if you get here in half an hour, he'll work you in."

"All right." Her hand trembled as she put the phone down. Something must be seriously wrong for Dr. Sanders to insist that she come in.

Or maybe not, she reassured herself. Maybe Nick had a vitamin deficiency or needed iron. Something like that. This could be just another instance of Dr. Sanders's personal interest in his patients. He always took extra time with kids. When Nick had suffered nightmares after Dean's death three years ago, Dr. Sanders had seen the boy several times just to listen to his fears and his sadness over the loss of his father. And last week the doctor had spent a good ten minutes with Nick, discussing the Yankees' chances of winning the pennant this year.

"Nothing to worry about," she told herself firmly as she started back to the living room. But her upbeat statement didn't banish the queasy feeling in the pit of her stomach.

She found Nick absorbed in moving pieces around the chess board. She didn't want to alarm him, too, so she hid her nerves behind a bright smile. "Change in plans, pal. I have to leave early. Pack up the chess set and you can play with Grandpa. I'm sure he'll appreciate your company." Her father was laid up after a knee replacement and was as bored as his grandson.

A sullen look that was becoming all too familiar settled on Nick's face. "I don't want to go to Grandma and Grandpa's. They don't let me watch *South Park.*"

"And neither do I, Mr. Brenner."

"Yeah, but—" He muttered "Oops" under his breath and looked away.

Mallory wondered if he got to watch the show she'd banned at one of his friends' homes, but she'd explore that later. "Hurry up, Nick. We need to get going."

"Why can't I stay home?"

"I guess I could call Angela and see if she can sit with you."

Nick threw another pillow to the floor. "I don't need a *babysitter.*" His voice rose. "I'm big enough to stay by myself."

"Not for three hours."

"If Dad was still alive, he'd let me."

That hurt. Mallory swallowed a tear and counted to ten. Since Nick had been ill, he'd tested limits and tried her patience constantly. "Don't go pushing my buttons, young man. Dad isn't here anymore and you're not to second-guess what he might've said. Now get your chessboard and let's go."

Scowling, Nick got to his feet and shuffled after her to the door. She dropped him off at her parents' with the admonition to "be nice," then drove to Dr. Sanders's office.

The waiting room was crowded, but Helena, Dr. Sanders's nurse, called her right in. A mother with two cranky preschoolers muttered something unpleasant as Mallory walked past, but Mallory ignored her. The knot of anxiety tightened in her chest. What could the doctor have to say that necessitated calling her in ahead of everyone else?

Helena pointed the way to the doctor's private office, but Mallory didn't need directions. She'd been coming here since she was a child herself. She went in, and he rose to take her hand and lead her to a small sofa. As she sat, the odor of cherry lollipops, a smell she always associated with this room, rose from the dish on the coffee table.

Dr. Sanders sat down beside her. Instead of beginning their conversation with a joke as he often did, today the doctor was silent and somber. The knot in Mallory's chest wrenched tighter as he picked up a sheet of paper from the coffee table. "We have the lab report from Nick's blood test," he said.

Though her mouth had gone dry, she swallowed. "Is something wrong?"

He set the paper down and leaned forward. Voice softer now, he said, "Nick's white blood count is extremely high."

"Does…that mean he has an infection? Or…"

Dr. Sanders covered her icy hand with his warm one. "I don't know an easy way to tell you this, Mallory. Nicholas has leukemia. Acute myelogenous leukemia."

The first two words of the diagnosis meant nothing to Mallory, but *leukemia*. She'd heard that word and from what she recalled, it meant…death.

She felt herself falling, sliding into a deep, dark hole. Though she still sat beside Dr. Sanders, still felt air moving in and out of her lungs, nothing around her seemed the same. Nothing seemed real. The sounds from the hallway faded, the hum of the air-conditioning stilled. Even her own body seemed alien. She saw that Dr. Sanders still held her hand, but she couldn't feel it. Her nerve endings had frozen.

"Leukemia," she muttered. "Cancer." She gritted her teeth. She had to hold herself together or she'd shatter into pieces like a broken glass. "Nick's going to… Is…is he going to die?"

Dr. Sanders shook his head and patted her hand. "No, leukemia isn't a death sentence anymore. The majority of children survive. But he needs treatment, and we'll see that he gets it."

She nodded. The thought of treatment gave her something tangible to concentrate on. "When can you start?"

"I don't have the training or the facilities here. He needs a cancer center, a specialist. Gaines Memorial in Houston is the closest and, fortunately, it's one of the top three in the country. I've already called to check on their admission procedures."

Houston. Away from her family, her friends. But that was inconsequential if the clinic there could help Nick. "How…how soon will we need to be there?"

"They want you there in three days."

So soon. "Is Nick…" Her voice faded, but she managed to whisper, "Is he in danger?"

"No immediate danger, but they do need to start as soon as possible."

His voice was reassuring. But, three days. And so much to get done. Her mind swam with fragments of a to-do list. Call Lauri…arrange for someone to help out at the shop…airline tickets…check her insurance policy… Thoughts jumped into her mind, flitted away.

She rose, sat down again. "I…I don't know anything about leukemia or how it's treated. I should check the Internet." She wondered if she'd have time.

Dr. Sanders nodded. "That's just what I expected you to say, and you're right. You need to be informed. This will give you an introduction." He handed her a pamphlet. "There's a list of books and Web sites, too."

"What about a doctor?" Mallory asked. "Who will we see?"

"The hospital gave me names of doctors on staff there. I can check them out and recommend one if you like."

"I'll trust you to pick the best."

"Would you like me to tell Nicholas?" he asked gently.

She hadn't even thought of that. "No, I'll tell him," she decided. "He's at my parents' now. They'll help. And afterward—tomorrow maybe—then you can talk to him, explain the…the illness."

Dr. Sanders nodded. "You're a strong woman, Mallory. You've had to be, losing Dean, raising Nicholas on your own and running a business. Your son is strong, too, and brave. What the two of you have to face won't be easy, but I have every confidence you'll get through it."

"Thank you." Though she could barely feel her legs, they apparently worked, because she crossed the room to the door. Dr. Sanders opened it for her, but she stopped, grasping at a last shred of hope. "Could there be a mistake? Could the lab report be wrong? Maybe Nick should have another blood test."

The doctor shook his head. "You'd just be wasting time."

Time. It could be Nick's ally…or his enemy. She wouldn't waste a minute. She hurried to the parking lot.

Her damp hands clutched the steering wheel as she drove toward her parents' home. They'd help. Her father, rabbi of Beth Jacob, Valerosa's only synagogue, had sustained his congregants through times of trouble, and he and her mother had been her chief support through the dark days after Dean's death. She'd lean on them now, and with their faith and courage to supplement hers, she prayed Nick would battle this illness and conquer it.

Half an hour later, sitting beside her son, Mallory took his hand. She forced her voice to stay steady. "Dr. Sanders found out what's making you so tired. You have an illness called leukemia."

She'd already told her parents the news. They'd been shocked, but they'd pulled together, and now she felt her mother's gentle hand on her shoulder. Nick's eyes widened and his fingers tightened around hers. But he surprised her and his grandparents by saying, "I knew something was wrong. I'm glad to know what it is."

Mallory blinked back tears. "The doctors who can help you are in Houston," she said, dreading the thought that he'd be away from everyone and everything he knew.

His brow furrowed. "Will I have to take shots?"

She swallowed. "I don't know. Maybe."

Her son squared his shoulders. "Then I guess I will if they'll get me well." A half smile appeared. "Can we go to an Astros game?" The Houston Astros were his second favorite team, after the Yankees.

"Sure we can. Houston has lots of things to do. We'll make it an adventure," Mallory said, and hoped they could.

"That'll be cool, seeing the Astros, huh, Grandpa?" Nick said.

Mallory's father nodded and smiled, but his face was still pale.

"I'll go to Houston with you," Lydia Roseman said, but Mallory shook her head. She hugged her mother.

"I appreciate the offer and I wish you could be there, but you need to be home with Dad." Although her father insisted he could manage on his own, Mallory would not be swayed. "If Nick...if *I* need you, then you'll come," she said, and finally they agreed.

"I need to go by the shop and talk to Lauri," Mallory said.

"Of course." Her father put his arm around her and walked her to the door.

"I'm scared," Mallory whispered.

"I know, but remember, 'For every mountain—'"

"'There is a miracle,'" Mallory finished, smiling through her tears. Her father collected quotes to build his sermons around. He had a proverb for every occasion and this was one of his favorites. "I'll remember," she promised.

Leaving Nick in her parents' loving hands, she hurried to the florist shop to tell her partner. Lauri hugged Mallory close. "Don't you worry about a thing. This store's way down on your priority list. There are plenty of college kids home for the summer who'd love to have a job in a nice, air-conditioned shop. Now, what can I do to help?"

They came up with a list, then Lauri shoved Mallory out the door. "Go home and don't show your face here anymore."

Grateful, Mallory went back to her parents' house. She found Nick playing with his Game Boy. That, she thought, was the best distraction for any child.

At dinner that evening they all joined hands around the table as her father led them in a prayer for Nick's recovery. The familiar Hebrew words comforted Mallory, and her father's voice, as deep and calm as it was in the synagogue, steadied her. For the first time since she'd heard the grim news, her frozen limbs seemed to thaw.

Still, she couldn't sleep that night. She wished for Dean, who'd been her rock for the eight years of their marriage. He'd been a wonderful husband and father. And when a drunk driver had hit his car head-on, she'd at least had the chance to tell him so. She'd held him in her arms in the hospital and told him how much she loved him…and then, in an instant, he was gone.

"Don't let me lose Nick, too," she prayed and vowed she'd fight this disease in every way she knew.

* * *

News spread quickly in a small town, and by the next afternoon, Mallory had dozens of calls with offers of help. Lauri's husband Mark offered to drive Mallory's car to Houston. She'd need it there, but she and Nick would fly in. Nick's fever and listlessness had returned, and Mallory didn't think he could handle a long car trip.

The members of her Torah study group already had a schedule for checking on her house and taking care of the yard. All that remained were the arrangements with the cancer specialist, and Dr. Sanders would let her know about that.

When they arrived for their appointment, he visited with Nick first, then called Mallory into his office.

"Have you found us a doctor?" she asked.

"Yes, he's young—well, young by my standards— but he's highly regarded."

"That's good to hear." Mallory reached into her purse for the notebook and pen she'd brought. "What's his name?"

"Berger. Dr. Kent Berger."

"Berg…" The pen dropped out of her hand. With the other hand she grasped the arm of the couch. Surely she'd heard wrong. "Wh-who?"

The doctor bent to retrieve the pen. "Kent Berger. Everyone I spoke to says he has a superb reputation. I'm putting you in capable hands."

Mallory bit the inside of her lip and suppressed the impulse to laugh hysterically. *Kent Berger.* She'd buried that name deep inside, never in eleven years allowed herself to speak it or even think it.

Dr. Sanders glanced at her sharply. "Is something wrong?"

Mallory shook her head. "I, um, just thought you'd have several names."

Dr. Sanders frowned. "You asked for the best. From what I hear, Berger *is* the best." He studied her face, glanced down at the trembling hands she hadn't thought to conceal. "Mallory, if something makes you uncomfortable about seeing this man, say so and make a change now." He looked at her thoughtfully. "Do you know him?"

"N-*no*," she said. "For a minute I thought the name sounded familiar, but…but I'm sure I was wrong." She clasped her hands together and fought to control her breathing.

The name was all too familiar. She knew him all too well. Kent Berger. Nick's…father.

Years had passed since she'd thought of him as the parent of her child. And now—

There couldn't be a worse time to face Kent Berger again.

Chapter Two

Dr. Sanders picked up a sheet of paper. "I've spoken with Dr. Berger's nurse, Catherine Garland. She wants you to call." He handed her the paper and rose.

Mallory stared at him blankly. What was she supposed to do? *Get up.* She got to her feet, watched the papers she held scatter over the coffee table. "Oh," she murmured.

Dr. Sanders looked concerned. "Mallory, are you all right? Do you need some water?"

"No, I'm…okay. Just stressed." She gathered the papers and stuffed them in her purse. With an effort, she pulled herself together and shook the doctor's hand. "Thank you for everything."

Dr. Sanders put his arm around her and walked her to the door. "Dr. Berger will keep me informed of Nick's progress, but if you want to ask questions or just talk, I'm a phone call away."

She hugged him. Voice breaking, she said, "I'll remember. Thanks."

She got Nick from the waiting room and drove home, and was surprised she could control the car, her hands shook so badly. *Kent Berger…Kent Berger…*

She remembered the first time she'd seen him. She'd had a summer job lifeguarding at the Comanche Trails Resort just outside of Valerosa. On that bright June morning her gaze swept over the Olympic-size swimming pool and stopped at the nearby high board, trapped by the sight of the man halfway up the ladder.

The morning sun shone on him, scattering chestnut highlights through his dark brown hair. He wasn't tall, perhaps a couple of inches under six feet, but his body was magnificent. Broad shoulders, wide chest covered with curly, dark hair, flat belly, thighs roped with muscle and not a spare ounce of flesh.

Her stare must have drawn him, for he turned his head. From her perch on the lifeguard chair, Mallory's eyes were even with his. Their gazes locked, and everything else faded—the noisy shouts and splashes of children, the odor of chlorine, the North Texas heat. She saw nothing but the dark eyes that captured hers, felt nothing but the sudden pounding of her heart.

He smiled, a slow, lazy curving of his mouth that she felt as intensely as if it had touched hers. Barely realizing what she was doing, she lifted a finger to trace her tingling lips. He held her gaze a moment longer, then continued up the ladder…and the world came back into focus.

He strode across the board, and Mallory held her

breath. He bounced, then rocketed through the air in a powerful jackknife. The breath left Mallory's lungs in a whoosh as he plunged downward and cut the water with barely a splash. He reminded her of some ancient god, plummeting from heaven to earth.

In a moment, he emerged from the water, swam to the side and pulled himself out. Shaking the drops from his hair, he glanced toward her…and winked. A warmth that owed nothing to the June sunshine spread through her body.

High-pitched shrieks distracted her, and she turned. Two toddlers were fighting over a toy sailboat. One grabbed the boat and darted away, heading toward the deep end of the pool, dangerously close to the edge.

Alarmed, Mallory scrambled down from her chair, but the man she'd been watching was ahead of her. He strode forward and blocked the little boy's path. Startled, the child stared up at what must have looked like a giant to him and began to wail. But the man squatted down to eye level with the little boy and said something to him. Within seconds, the child's tears vanished and he broke into a grin. The man took his hand and led him back to his mother.

Most guys would have cringed at facing a screaming two-year-old, but not this man. Later, Mallory learned he was a pediatrician….

Wait a minute, Mallory thought now as she braked for a red light. The Kent Berger she'd known wasn't a cancer specialist in Houston. He was a pediatrician in Chicago. Of course! This *had* to be a different man.

Relieved at the idea, she drove home, turned on the TV and settled Nick on the living room couch with his ever-present remote, then went into the kitchen and pulled the slip of paper with the nurse's name and the office phone number out of her purse.

As soon as she heard Catherine Garland's voice, Mallory knew she was in good hands. Catherine explained that their stay in Houston might be as long as several months. "But you don't need to worry about living arrangements. The clinic maintains an apartment complex right around the corner where families can stay."

She could cross that off her list. "My son won't have to be in the hospital?"

"Probably for a few days. You'll come to the clinic first, so Nick can have additional blood work and bone marrow testing. We do as much as we can on an outpatient basis. We believe in keeping lives as normal as possible during treatment."

"I'm glad to hear that." Perhaps the Astros game wasn't as far-fetched as she'd thought. "What about Dr. Berger? When will he see Nick?"

"When the tests are finished. He's out of town now but he should be back the day you arrive."

Even though she'd convinced herself he wasn't the man she knew, she had to ask. "I'd like to know more about him."

"He's wonderful, and I'm not saying that because I work for him. You can ask anyone. He's truly the best."

"But how is he with kids? My son has had the same doctor nearly all his life, and I'm...well, I'm a little nervous about how he'll react to a stranger."

"Oh, Dr. Berger will win him over right away. He specializes in children's cancer. He was a pediatrician before he started working with cancer patients."

"Where?" *Let her say Boise or Anchorage or some-place I've never heard of.*

"Chicago."

Mallory sank into a chair. He was *that* Kent Berger after all.

She managed to thank Catherine and disconnect before the phone fell from her shaking hands and clattered to the floor.

"What was that?" Nick called from the living room.

"Nothing." She bent down and retrieved the phone. "It doesn't matter who he is," she whispered. All that mattered was that he could make Nick well. She set the phone on the counter and went into the small room she used as a home office.

She sat down at the computer and typed in Kent's name. Funny, she'd never even imagined doing that before. She'd closed the door on Kent Berger years ago just as he had on her. She'd never let herself wonder where he was and if he were doing something important. Now she had to know.

The search engine turned up dozens of articles in medical journals, some she even recognized, like the *New England Journal of Medicine.* He'd given seminars and interviews to the media and was considered one of the top specialists in the U.S. on childhood leukemia—acute myelogenous leukemia, Nick's type, in particular.

So it didn't matter that she knew him, that she'd once thought she'd spend the rest of her life with him. It didn't even matter that he'd lied to her about their future. She could handle seeing Kent again. All that was important was that he could make Nick well.

He probably wouldn't even remember her. She'd been a brief diversion for him, nothing more. To him, their love affair hadn't been a life-changing event. He didn't know the aftermath of that long ago summer—Nick.

Should she tell him? *No,* she thought fiercely. If he found out Nick was his child, he'd turn Nick's care over to someone else, someone who might be only second best. This wasn't about Kent's rights; it was about Nick's. And with her son's life at stake, she couldn't take chances.

Kent Berger may have given Nick life, but he hadn't been Nick's parent. But now, please, God, he'd make up for that. He'd save the life of the son he would never know he'd fathered.

Two days later, sitting in her son's hospital room at Gaines Memorial, Mallory watched Nick's small chest move up and down. Worn out from yesterday's plane trip and the clinic visit this morning, he'd fallen asleep as soon as he'd gotten into bed. He'd been stoic in the face of technicians bearing needles and residents poking and prodding, but Mallory had to admit that the clinic itself had a lot to do with his bravery. For a place that specialized in children who were sick, it was remarkably cheerful and welcoming.

As Catherine predicted, Nick was admitted to the hospital that afternoon. Mallory hated hospitals—the sounds, the smells—but she chose to view Gaines Memorial as a battle station in the war against Nick's disease. She would not let the environment depress her, or Nick, either. She hung up the New York Yankees banner he'd brought along, and as soon as she could, she went down to the gift shop and bought a painting of bright yellow chrysanthemums and a grinning stuffed monkey to liven up his room.

Now Mallory glanced at her watch. Still a long time before the doctor was due. She intended to think of Kent Berger as "the doctor," or if necessary as "Dr. Berger, without a first name." Nothing personal. She would not remember summer nights in his arms, the taste of his lips, or the scent of his skin.

She stood and paced the small room. If she was jittery, she had every right. Today, or tomorrow at the latest, the verdict on her son's future would be delivered.

She had plenty of time to call her parents, Dean's parents, and Lauri and let them know how the day had gone. With another glance at Nick to assure herself he slept peacefully, she left the room, found a small waiting area down the hall and took out her cell phone. She checked to be sure she could use her cell in this area of the hospital, then dialed.

Her calls took a good fifteen minutes. She had so much to say, and yet so little. But she could give the people waiting at home some reassurance. She'd brought Nick to a good place. She hung up and, trying to ignore her aching feet, headed back to his room.

A nurse hurried out of his door. Was something wrong? Propelled by fear, Mallory dashed forward, then halted in the doorway, unable to take another step, as a hauntingly familiar voice reached her ears.

He sat by the bed, his head bent close to Nick's. He was talking baseball and he had the boy's full attention.

He must have come directly from the airport because he wore a white dress shirt that contrasted starkly with his tanned skin. His shoulders were slightly broader than she remembered, his chest wider, but no gray marred the thick, dark hair. The hand that lay lightly on the bed rails was the same, too—lean, strong.

He hadn't changed. And oh, God, she'd never realized how much Nick looked like him. The shape of his face, the way he cocked his head to listen, even the half smile. She'd never let herself notice. Would *he?*

Please, no, she begged. She must have made a sound of supplication, because he looked up.

And for the first time in eleven years, she stared into his eyes.

Chapter Three

He didn't recognize her.

His expression was cordial, but she saw no hint of awareness in his gaze.

What made her think he would remember? What made her believe she'd meant enough to him to remain in his mind? Pride forced her to square her shoulders and step into the room. She'd deal with her feelings of hurt and anger later. What mattered now was Nick.

As she came into the room, Kent smiled and extended his hand. "Mrs. Bren——"

His hand froze in midair. He glanced at the chart on the stand beside him, then up again. "*Mallory* Brenner...Mallory *Roseman?*"

Her breath backed up in her lungs. He did remember her after all. Silently, she nodded.

"You...cut your hair," he blurted, his words seeming to surprise him as much as they did her. His cheeks flushed, and abruptly his eyes swung back to his hand, still suspended. He reached out and, reluctantly, Mallory did the same.

Their hands met above the bed where Nicholas— where their *son*—lay staring at them with curiosity. "You guys know each other?"

"We did, years ago," Mallory muttered and managed a casual shrug. She hoped she communicated that whatever had happened between them was inconsequential and done with long ago. Realizing she still grasped Kent's hand, she let it go and stepped back. What she needed now was his medical skill. "About Nick—" she began.

"Yes. Why don't you sit down," Kent suggested, "and we'll talk about what happens next."

His voice was calming, and Mallory remembered again the little boy he'd spoken to at the pool that long-ago summer morning. She took a chair beside the bed.

Kent turned to Nick. "Nick, you've had some people sticking you today, and they tell me you've been very brave."

"Is the sticking over?" Nick asked.

"I'm afraid not. Tomorrow morning you're going to have a spinal tap." Gently, matter-of-factly, he explained the procedure.

Nick's hand slid to Mallory's and clasped it tightly, but his eyes were glued to Kent's. When Kent asked if he understood, he nodded. "I won't cry," he said. "At least I'll try not to."

"Good," Kent said, smiling at him. "And I won't

spring any surprises on you. Whatever we have to do to lick this illness, I'll tell you beforehand. Is that a deal?"

"Deal," the boy said, and Mallory saw with relief that Kent had won his trust.

Kent turned to her now. "The usual course of treatment for AML, Nick's type of leukemia, is several rounds of chemotherapy, then a transplant…"

"Transplant?" She didn't know much about transplants except that there was always a chance of rejection.

Kent seemed to sense her fear. "Transplants are getting to be commonplace in many types of cancer," he said reassuringly. "You'll meet lots of kids who've had them and are doing quite well."

Calmer now, Mallory nodded.

"Tomorrow afternoon," Kent continued, "I'll go over the results of the tests and talk more about the treatment with you and Nick…and Nick's father." He glanced toward the door. "Is he here with you?"

Mallory didn't allow herself to wince at the phrase *Nick's father.* "My husband died three years ago," she said flatly.

Something flashed in Kent's eyes, disappeared. "I'm sorry. I met him, I believe." Without glancing at the chart, he said, "Dean," and Mallory nodded.

He picked up Nick's chart. "See you tomorrow, pal," he said and ruffled the boy's hair.

When he left, Mallory let out a long breath. She was over the worst. She'd survived the first meeting. From now on she'd be fine, as long as they didn't dredge up old memories that might lead to dangerous questions. And why should they? They were doctor, patient and patient's mother. She suspected Kent would want to keep it that way as much as she did. Besides, he surely had a life beyond the hospital. Eleven years had passed. He must have a wife and…and children.

"Mom." Nick's voice brought her out of her reverie.

"Yes, hon."

"How do you know Doctor Berger?"

Trust her inquisitive son to ask. "He, uh, spent a summer in Valerosa a long time ago. I met him then."

Nick eyed her with interest. "Was that before I was born?"

About nine months, she thought with a pang. "Uh-huh."

"Did you like him?"

Mallory felt heat rise to her cheeks. "Yes, he was very nice."

"I like him, too," Nick said. "I'm glad he's going to be my doctor."

On that, she could agree. "Me, too."

"He's going to make me well," her son said, with total confidence.

Mallory bit her lip. Oh, God, she hoped so. "Yes, he is. Now, why don't you get some sleep? You have a big day tomorrow." She bent to fluff his pillow and drop a kiss on his forehead.

He caught her hand. "Mommy."

Rarely did Nick call her Mommy anymore. He'd pronounced himself too big for that several years ago. She squeezed his hand. "Yes?"

"Will you sit here by me till I get to sleep?"

"I'd like that," Mallory said, "and maybe we could hold hands, okay?"

"Yeah."

Mallory kept watch as he shut his eyes and fell asleep.

Only when the room was still did she allow her thoughts to drift back to Kent. He'd turned out to be the doctor she always imagined he'd be, with a bedside manner worthy of Albert Schweitzer. But why did he have to look like every woman's fantasy lover?

Why couldn't he have lost his hair or developed a paunch? That would make things so much easier.

Whack.

Kent served the ball against the wall of the racquetball court and when Stan Ferguson returned the shot, whipped it back with another satisfying smack. He slammed the ball again and again, the whoosh of air loud in his ears.

Mallory. Why did she have to be as pretty as ever, her mouth still so enticing, so kissable? Why couldn't she have turned into a hag?

"Point," Stan called. "Hey, man, you're killing me. You're up thirteen-two."

"Yeah," Kent muttered. Ordinarily if he beat Stan by this much, he'd be elated. Now he only focused on the force of his arm, the slap of the ball against wood.

Why hadn't he taken time to look at the boy's chart more carefully yesterday? He'd rushed in from the airport with barely enough time to read the test results, so he hadn't glanced at the parents' names. He'd gotten a monumental shock when he'd recognized the mother.

Stan missed a ball, then another.

"Game over." Kent caught the ball and bounced it, then tossed it and the racquet into his gym bag.

"Hey, good buddy, you're on a tear today," Stan said as they walked off the court. "Letting out some anger, are we?"

Kent managed a laugh as he stared straight ahead. "Remind me never to play racquetball with a psychiatrist."

"We can't help noticing displays of emotion. One of the drawbacks of the profession. Last time I saw you murder the ball that way was when you and Lisa divorced."

"Spare me the psychoanalysis." Kent swiped a towel over his sweaty face. "What you saw isn't anger, it's athletic skill."

They halted in front of the showers, and Stan gave him a penetrating look. "Well, if you ever want to talk about your newfound 'skill,' you can have a discount."

"Not necessary, but thanks." He pulled the damp T-shirt over his head. He'd feel foolish spilling his guts about an affair that ended years ago.

"Have time for lunch later?" Stan asked.

"Not today. Too busy." Kent tossed his shorts aside and stepped into the shower. He turned the water on full force and let it pour over him. Damn, he hated being so transparent, but running into Mallory after all this time brought back memories and emotions he thought he'd put to rest years ago.

Getting over her hadn't been easy. No, it had been tough facing the fact that she'd played him for a fool, used him as bait to snag Dean Brenner. Remembering his last phone call to her, he shut his eyes as icy water droplets stung him as if they were needles.

He'd called from the hospital in Rome, three weeks after he'd planned on returning to Valerosa. She'd have been back at school in Lubbock by then. But when he called her dorm, he learned she wasn't enrolled that semester. Surprised and worried, he tried her at home.

"Mallory?" A deep, rich laugh sounded over the wire

and Ophelia, the Rosemans' housekeeper, said, "She's not here. That girl's done gone and got herself married."

Staggered, he gasped, "Married? When? Who?"

"Few days ago. Married Dean Brenner. I always knew those two'd wake up someday and see they was meant for each other. Been hangin' around together since they was little tykes."

She paused. "You want their number in El Paso?"

For some reason, he wrote it down, hung up, then sat back and stared unseeing out the window. After a minute he glanced at the slip of paper in his hand, crumbled it into a ball and tossed it in the trash.

Kent opened his eyes. Didn't matter now. Couldn't. Both of them had one very sick kid to worry about. Nick was their only connection.

The next night, Mallory tiptoed out of Nick's room and made her way down the hall to the waiting area. She bypassed an armchair, sat on the window ledge and stared into the night. It was 1:00 a.m., and lights were still on all over the medical center. Hospitals never slept.

She leaned her forehead against the glass. Today had been the worst day since Nick had gotten sick, even worse somehow than the afternoon Dr. Sanders had told her he had leukemia.

She'd felt so optimistic when she awoke this morning. Kent—Dr. Berger—had explained that AML was nearly always amenable to chemotherapy. The transplant, whether of bone marrow or stem cells, would come later, but first things first. The chemo would begin immediately.

She was proud of the way Nick reacted. He said he

and his mom planned to beat this disease, then asked when he'd be out of the hospital. His grin broke out when Kent—Dr. Berger—said probably in a few days, as soon as they saw how he tolerated the chemo.

Tolerated? Mallory thought bitterly. Such a bland word. The nurses had told her reactions to chemo could vary from mild to severe, but only now did she realize what "severe" meant. Nick had first developed an excruciating headache, then nausea so fierce he screamed every time it gripped him. The nurse said the doctor would adjust the dose next time. How could they have been so far off? How could Nick—and she—endure a next time?

Oh, it hurt to see her baby so sick. And not to be able to help. All she could do was hold his hand.

For the first time she wondered if they'd come to the right place. Maybe they should have gone to Sloan-Kettering in New York or another big cancer center. At least there she wouldn't have the added stress of wondering if Nick's doctor had noticed the boy's birthday and done the math.

Tears slid down her cheeks and dampened the windowpane. She was homesick. She wanted someone to lean on.

A hand touched her shoulder.

Startled, she turned. And met Kent's eyes.

Damn, Kent thought, he hadn't meant to touch her, but he'd seen her at the window, shoulders slumped. Her son's reaction to his first dose of chemo had to be tough for her. He'd decided to stop and reassure her, as he'd do for any parent. A brief word of explanation and sympathy, and he'd be on his way.

She'd been crying. He saw the sheen of tears in her eyes as she turned.

For the first time in his medical career, he couldn't think of the right words. He settled for, "Rough day."

"Too rough." Pain and accusation shone through her tears. "He shouldn't have to be so sick. Can't you tell ahead of time what dose he needs?"

"No, reactions vary. Sometimes a child will tolerate one dose, then the next time react poorly to the very same one."

"So we can expect more of the same?"

He sighed. "Maybe." He saw her swallow, and added, "I won't sugarcoat this, Mallory."

She bit her lip. "No, of course not."

"Once Nick is out of the hospital and you're settled at the apartment complex, you'll meet other families. You'll have a built-in support system."

She brushed away the tears that stained her cheeks and nodded. "That'll help."

It would, of course. And *he* shouldn't get personally involved. He should leave it right there, turn away from her, go home and crash. But he found himself saying, "Walk down to the doctors' lounge with me. I bet you haven't eaten. We'll find you a snack."

"Oh, no. I couldn't eat a thing."

Another opportunity to back off. Instead he said, "Join me then, while I have something. Come on."

She glanced back down the hall toward her son's room. "But what if he—?"

"He won't wake up. He's sleeping like a log." At her questioning look, he said, "I looked in on him."

"Oh, well, then…" She rose and brushed her hair

back from her face. It was a gesture he remembered from long ago.

They walked down the hall silently, Kent automatically adjusting his stride to hers.

The lounge was dim and empty. Kent didn't bother turning on the overhead light. Instead he flipped on a small light over the counter. They'd only be here a few minutes. He'd make himself some tea, insist she have a cup, too, then get out of here. That'd be five…okay, seven minutes tops.

He grabbed two plastic cups, filled them with water and put them in the microwave. Mallory sat at the table, waiting. He used to imagine meeting her again and letting his anger spew out as he confronted her about the ending of their relationship. But now, when she was worn out and frightened, wasn't the time. He fixed the tea, got some packets of cheese and crackers out of the cabinet and sat down across from her.

She shook her head at the food. "Eat," he said firmly. "You have to stay strong."

"Okay, doc." She used to call him that, her voice teasing. She must remember, too, he thought as he saw her cheeks redden. She stared at the crackers, unwrapping them carefully, then methodically folding the paper. She picked up a cracker, took a bite and grimaced.

"Eat," he repeated.

She nodded, dutifully finished the cracker and sipped her tea.

Kent put his cup down. "Tell me about Nick."

Her shoulders tensed, and she looked at him for a moment, as if gauging the reason for his question. Then she let out a breath. "He's a typical ten-year-old. He does pretty well in school, loves math, likes reading and would like writing, too, if it weren't for punctuation. He plays Little League, and he's really good. This spring he led his team in home runs before he—" her voice trembled "—got sick." She looked up, and tears welled in her eyes. "Will he…will he be able to play again?"

Kent sighed. "There are no guarantees, but the chances are good. Maybe not this year, but eventually."

"Then I can hope for that." She smiled but he sensed it was forced. "At least he can watch baseball on TV."

"The Yankees."

Her eyes flew to his, and she tensed again. "Yes, how do you know?"

"He told me. We were talking after I examined him this morning."

"He wants to grow up to be Rick Howard."

"Reminds me of myself at the same age, only I wanted to be Reggie Jackson." Kent smiled, but Mallory didn't smile back. Instead, she stared into her tea cup. She picked it up, but her hand shook and she set it back on the table.

Hoping to distract her, Kent changed the subject. "How are your parents?"

"They're fine. They'd have been here but my dad's recuperating from a knee replacement."

"I'm sorry. I know that's a painful operation. I'm sure they're here in spirit."

"Yes. I have a lot of support from back home. My business partner, Lauri Gold—"

"You have a business?"

She smiled. "A florist shop. Buds and Blossoms."

"I'm surprised. If I remember correctly, you talked about going into psychology."

"If I'd gone with that, I'd still be in school."

Her perfume wafted across the table to him. The same scent she'd always worn. He cleared his throat. "Hard to be in school with a kid to raise."

"Yes."

"You've done a good job, Mallory. Nick's a great kid."

"Thanks."

He wanted to keep her talking, to know about the Mallory of today, so he asked more questions. The room was quiet, strangely intimate, and he felt the pain and outrage he'd carried all these years slipping away. Melting in the warmth of her presence. Maybe this was one of the vivid dreams he used to have of her, dreams that left him aching, wanting.

Finally, she glanced at her watch. "It's after two." She stifled a yawn. "Won't your wife worry?"

"My...? I'm divorced."

She stared at him for a long, charged moment, then dropped her gaze. "I'd, um, better get back to Nick's room." She began gathering the cups.

"Sure." He helped her clear the table, and they walked back together.

She stopped in the doorway to Nick's room. "Talking to you helped a lot," she said softly. "Thanks for getting me through this night." She reached out, almost touched his arm, then abruptly dropped her hand. "Good night."

"Good night."

Mallory stepped inside the room, listened as Kent's footsteps receded down the hall, then shut the door. *Divorced,* she thought as the full implication sank in. *Oh, no.*

Chapter Four

Two days later, Mallory sat in Nick's room, entering information in her laptop. She'd met several other mothers of young cancer patients, and one had suggested she keep a daily log of Nick's progress.

Nick was feeling better. This afternoon he was engrossed in a baseball game on TV. "Not the Yankees," he'd complained, "but better than nothin'."

"Noth*ing,*" Mallory corrected automatically.

"Aw, Mom."

As she continued typing, Mallory heard the commentator say, "A high pop fly to short right field."

"Come on, get it," Nick urged.

Mallory looked up, pleased by the excitement in his voice.

She glanced at the TV screen. The right fielder jogged in, lifted a glove and bobbled the ball.

"Aw, man, can't you hold on to the ball, you jerk?"

"Nick," Mallory chided. "Watch your language."

"Geez, Mom. Don't you ever get excited about a ball game?"

"Never…well, hardly ever."

"Dad did."

"I know," Mallory sighed, as the next batter struck out.

"Sure. You and Dad knew each other forever." He grinned when she glanced up at him. "Tell me the story of how you met."

Her fingers poised on the keyboard. "I thought you were watching the game."

"Mom, hel-*lo*. End of inning. Commercial break."

"You've heard the story a hundred times."

"Yeah, but I like it better than listening to someone go on about oatmeal." He pointed to the screen, where a family was cheerfully devouring their breakfast, and broke into the endearing little-boy grin she loved.

How could she turn him down? She saved her file and turned the computer off. "Okay, when your grandpa became the rabbi at Beth Jacob and we moved to Valerosa, our house was across the street from your Brenner grandparents. The first morning we were there I went outside to check out the neighborhood when I saw this kid across the street, scowling at me."

"What did he say?"

"He said, 'My mom said the new rabbi has a kid named Mallory. Are *you* Mallory?' And when I said yes, he said, 'I thought Mallory was a boy's name. You're a girl.'"

"Yeah, he was disappointed."

"He was, but I fixed him. I chomped my gum, blew the biggest bubble I could and popped it, and then I said, 'Yeah, so what? I can run as fast as you.'"

Nick chuckled. "And he said, 'Prove it.' And you beat him to the corner."

"Well, almost. It was a tie, but I guess he was impressed because he said, 'You're not bad for a girl. Wanna see my bug collection?'"

"And you said, 'Sure, got any scorpions?'"

"I did, and from then on, we were best friends."

"And you grew up, got married and had me and lived happily ever after, well, until—" He broke off and turned. "Oh, hi, Dr. Berger."

"Hi, pal."

"We were talking about my dad," Nick said as Kent strode into the room and sat beside the bed. "Did you know him, too?"

"I did," he said evenly and shot a glance at Mallory. The warmth and caring she'd seen the other night in the doctors' lounge were gone. Today his gaze was cold, almost angry. Why? What did *he* have to be mad about? Surely he couldn't be jealous that she'd married Dean, not after all the promises *he'd* made and broken.

"Feeling better, hmm?" Kent asked Nick. When the boy nodded, he said, "We're going to give you another chemo dose tomorrow."

Nick's face fell. "The one the other day made me awful sick. Do you have to?" His voice trembled, and Mallory pulled her chair closer to the bed.

"Yeah, we do," Kent said, his voice gentle.

"Remember you told me you and your mom were going to beat this disease?"

Nick swallowed. "Yeah, the two of us, we're a team."

"Well, I'm on the team now, too. You could say I'm the manager." He put his hand on the boy's shoulder. "The opposing team has these blasts—big, fat white blood cells they're using against us—and the chemo zaps them." Mallory saw that Kent had Nick's full attention as he continued. "We've adjusted the chemo so you won't be as sick this time, but we have to use it. It's our strongest weapon. Okay, pal?"

"Okay," Nick said in a small voice.

"Good. See you tomorrow." He rose. "Nine-thirty."

Kent left the room without speaking to Mallory and strode toward the nurses' station. Resentment seethed in his veins. The anger that had dwindled the other evening had returned full force when he'd overheard the conversation about the happy Brenner family.

He stopped at the counter and made an entry on Nicholas's chart. He'd spent many sleepless nights wondering about Mallory's marriage to Dean Brenner. How "sudden" was it? How much had been in the works even while Mallory was supposedly in love with *him?*

She was here now and one day when her son was better, he'd ask the questions. And by God, before she left Houston, he'd have some answers.

Mallory paged through a copy of *Good Housekeeping* as she sat in the waiting room of the clinic. After only a minimal reaction to his second dose of chemo, Nick had been discharged from the hospital. Mallory was relieved. Not only was Nick feeling a little better, but she only had to encounter Kent once a week when he checked Nick and went over the results of blood tests.

She and Nick had settled into their two-bedroom apartment, and Nick had immediately made friends with Jeremy Spellman, another ten-year-old, who had been in treatment only two weeks longer than he. Mallory and Jeremy's mother Tamara and several other moms had bonded, too. No one could better understand what they were going through than other parents experiencing the same fears and hopes.

Nick had told her that he and Jeremy were designing a video game. Now they were seated, heads together, giggling as they drew on a piece of typing paper. Mallory listened.

"…and the monster Leukemator is waiting at the end of the tunnel," Jeremy said.

"Yeah, and he sends his blasts out to destroy Battleforce Bazooka."

"But Doctor Bergermaster has a secret weapon. It's…um, let's see, it's…Cheem."

"Cheem, the Extreme," Nick said. "Hey, Jer, this is really good. We should show it to Dr. Berger. Maybe he'll have some ideas to improve it."

"Maybe he could test it out on his own kids," Jeremy suggested.

"Nope, he doesn't have any kids."

Mallory frowned. How did Nick know *that?*

An hour later, as they left the clinic and headed for the exit, she asked him.

"Oh, we talk when he's checking me over. I asked him."

"Why?"

Her voice came out sharper than she intended and

Nick said, "I just wondered, that's all. You're sure cranky today."

"Sorry. How about I make it up to you?" she offered. "Since you're feeling better and your blood counts are up, we could go out to dinner. I'll treat you to McDonald's."

"Cool."

"Let's do it, then." She'd have to be careful not to let her emotional reactions to Kent affect the way she behaved with Nick.

They left the building and were heading across the parking lot just as Kent emerged from another door. Mallory grimaced. *Think of the devil, and he appears.* And her heart leaped at the sight of him, just as it had years ago. She kept her eyes straight ahead.

Her son, bless his heart, didn't. "Hey, Dr. Berger," he called and stopped. When Kent came alongside them, Nick said, "Guess what. We're going out to dinner, to McDonald's. Wanna come?"

Mallory jumped in quickly. "Nick, I'm sure Dr. Berger has things to do—"

"Nothing on the calendar for tonight," Kent said. "I'd love to join you." He flashed his killer smile, the rat. "My car's right over there. I'll follow you home and we can go together."

"Oh, that's not nec—"

"Wow! You have a Jaguar. Mom, is that awesome or what?"

"Awesome," Mallory muttered. If anything, the car vaulted Kent even higher in Nick's pantheon of heroes...that is, if a higher position were available. Dr. Bergermaster was, after all, already the leader of Battleforce Bazooka.

Saying nothing, she steered Nick to their own car, not at all surprised when her son groused, "*Our* car is so *nothin'*. We should get something classier."

"Sure," she said. "I'll put us on the list for a Ferrari as soon as we're back in Valerosa."

As she drove the few blocks to the apartment, Mallory pondered Kent's acceptance of Nick's invitation. Surely this wasn't standard procedure for a busy doctor to go out for fast food with one of his patients. She chewed on her bottom lip as she glanced in the rearview mirror at the sleek black Jaguar behind them. Did he have some inkling that Nick was more than just a patient?

Her hands tightened on the steering wheel. For the thousandth time, she asked herself why she'd come to Houston. Didn't she have enough to worry about without this fear lurking in the back of her mind? And for the thousandth time the same answer came. She wanted the best for Nick, and Kent was the best.

She'd just be cautious around him.

She pulled into her parking space and shook her head in disbelief as Nick fairly leaped out of their car and trotted over to Kent's. Nick hadn't had this much energy since he'd gotten sick. She followed slowly, hoping Nick would get into the front seat of the Jaguar beside Kent. Instead he hopped into the back and left the passenger seat for her.

Resigned, she got in. As she fastened her seat belt, she caught a whiff of Kent's cologne. Sandalwood. Masculine, sexy—oh, dear.

She let Nick do most of the talking as they drove to the nearest McDonald's. He had plenty to say, of course, chattering excitedly about the "awesome" car, his collection of model cars and the video game he and Jeremy were designing.

They slid to a stop in front of McDonald's and Kent got out of the car. By the time Mallory had unfastened her seat belt and picked up her purse, he'd come around to her side and opened the door for her. Always the gentleman, he extended his hand to help her out. She remembered how impressed she'd been with his manners the summer they'd been together. Today she ignored his hand. Manners were all surface, she told herself. What was important was inside. And Kent had let her down when it really mattered. She would keep that in mind and not allow his sexy cologne and beguiling smile to sweep her off her feet again. She was older and wiser than she'd been eleven years ago.

Nick scrambled out and glanced around the parking lot. "We've got the best car here," he announced.

Of course, Mallory thought. How many prominent physicians patronized fast-food restaurants?

Inside, they gave their orders, and Kent reached in his pocket. "I'll get it," he said.

"No, thank you."

Kent shrugged, and she thought she saw a hint of amusement in his eyes. *Let him laugh.* She would *not* allow this to become a...she wasn't sure what, but letting him pay for their meal seemed a step toward a more personal relationship. A complication she couldn't dare to encourage.

They carried their trays to a booth and sat down. She continued to let Nick carry the conversation, relieved at first and then concerned that he and Kent had so much to talk about.

Nick ate half his burger, then pushed it away. His appetite was still poor. Tonight hers wasn't much better. She nibbled at her food, wishing the meal over so they could leave.

But Nick was eyeing the outside playground. "Can I go out, Mom?" he asked.

Mallory hesitated, worried that he might overextend himself. And she didn't want to be alone with Kent. "I don't think—"

Sensing defeat, Nick said, "Let's ask Dr. Berger." He turned to Kent.

"Ten minutes," Kent said. "If you get tired sooner, come back. Your body will tell you when it's had enough."

"Thanks." Flashing a triumphant grin, he left them.

Alone.

Mallory began gathering up their leftovers. If she walked to the trash can really slowly, she could use up maybe two minutes. *Coward.* But she had reason to be afraid.

"I'll get us some coffee," Kent said.

"Thank you."

"Still take yours with two sugars?"

She nodded, surprised he remembered. With another man, she'd be flattered. With Kent—

She deposited their trash in the container and returned to the booth. Kent set the cups on the table and slid in across from her. Her hand closed around the coffee cup. His was inches away, close enough to reach for, to touch. She remembered the feel of his fingers clasping hers, the warmth of his palm...

"The first time we went out, I took you to the Burger Bar," he said softly.

She remembered, of course. Everything about that first afternoon was as vivid in her mind as events of the past week—the smell of broiling meat, the jukebox playing Whitney Houston's "I Will Always Love You," the heady excitement that Kent had noticed her and actually asked her out.

"Is the Burger Bar still there?" he asked.

She nodded, stirred her coffee. "I wasn't supposed to go out with you," she blurted.

He frowned. "Really? Why?"

"You were a guest at Comanche Trails. Employees weren't allowed to socialize with guests." Yet without a qualm, she'd said yes the minute he asked. She, the rabbi's daughter who never broke rules, hadn't given the restriction a second thought. And that was only the first rule she'd broken.

Kent's lips curved into the slow smile Mallory used to adore. "I didn't know that. I'm glad you decided to go."

Mallory didn't answer. Couldn't.

What if she'd stuck with her usual behavior and said no when he asked her out? She'd have avoided all the grief, all the anguish.

But she wouldn't have Nick.

She glanced out the window at her son, who was talking to another youngster on the playground. She'd endure everything she'd gone through again because of him. She glanced back at Kent and found him watching her thoughtfully, a half smile on his face. "What?" she asked.

"After we left the Burger Bar, you took me to see a prairie dog town."

Mallory laughed, half-embarrassed that she'd thought such an unsophisticated outing would impress a man who'd spent his last four years in Chicago. But he'd kissed her there, on that sun-scorched afternoon, with a chorus of tiny creatures chattering in the background and the whistle of a train sounding from somewhere far away.

She'd fallen in love that hot June day, and those same feelings, long buried, were stirring now. Again. *Fool. Now you know better.*

Abruptly she said, "How long were you married?"

He blinked at the sudden change of subject. "Three years."

"What happened?"

Kent hesitated, then answered, "Lisa and I were a bad match."

Curious now, she asked, "In what way?"

"We wanted different things. I met Lisa in New York when I was at Sloan-Kettering. She was a model. Then when we moved here, she had some offers and…she didn't want to spoil her body having children."

Mallory studied him thoughtfully. "Would you have sacrificed *your* career for children?"

"Yes," he said.

His voice rang with such intensity, his eyes shone with such pain that Mallory was staggered. Beneath the table she clenched her hands, which had suddenly gone cold. If he wanted a child this much, didn't he deserve to know that Nick was his?

Chapter Five

Say it, she thought. *He needs to know. Kent, you do have a child. Nick is yours....*

How would he react? He'd be shocked, of course, but what else? Would he be thrilled? Angry?

Heart drumming in her ears, she sat poised to speak, to tell the truth that would change Kent's life...and Nick's. But her vocal cords seemed frozen, her lips unable to move.

Once said, she could never take the words back. And far more important than Kent's reaction was how they would affect Nick.

Kent would refuse to continue treating Nick. A doctor might stitch up his son's cut lip, but he'd never treat his own child for cancer.

How would her son feel, getting a new physician?

Would he be as cooperative when someone else performed the painful bone marrow aspirations he required?

Kent might insist on telling Nick he was his father. That could be a disaster. After only a short time as his patient, Nick worshiped Kent. As a *doctor,* not as a parent. If he learned the truth, the shock and stress might affect his progress. How could she take that chance?

She stared down at her napkin, folded it in half, folded it again, into smaller and smaller pieces.

Kent put his hand over hers. "Mallory, I know you're worried, but Nick is making good progress. He's tolerating the chemo...."

Of course Kent assumed she was worrying about Nick. She looked up and managed a smile. "I know."

Kent gazed at her with such kindness. She swallowed a tear. "Kent, I—"

"Hey, Mom."

She jumped at the sound of Nick's voice and jerked her hand out of Kent's hold. Too late to tell him now, she thought with relief. Someday she'd tell him. Later, when Nick was well. After Kent had made him well. When the consequences wouldn't be so drastic.

"About ready to head home?" she asked Nick, noting how pale and tired he looked.

"Yeah, I think so."

Kent had been right. Nick's body had told him he'd had enough.

They gathered their cups and napkins and headed for the door. "Wait for me a minute," Mallory said, turning toward the restroom. She needed some time to collect herself.

In the ladies room she splashed water on her face,

then glanced in the mirror as she dried off. There were circles under her eyes. She looked as pale and drawn as Nick. She freshened her lipstick, but that didn't help much. She sighed, tossed the paper towel away and pushed open the door.

Kent and Nick stood waiting near the exit. Outside, a woman carrying a baby with one arm and holding a toddler's hand with the other approached the door. Nick noticed, opened the door and held it for her. Pleased, Mallory smiled to herself. All those lessons in manners she'd drummed into him had apparently stuck.

"Thank you." The woman smiled at Nick, then turned to Kent. "Your son is a sweetheart."

Your son. Mallory's hand flew to her mouth as Kent nodded and murmured a thank-you. *Oh, God,* Mallory thought. The words she couldn't say a few minutes ago...

Would the stranger's offhand remark cause Kent to notice Nick's resemblance to him? And then would he figure out their relationship himself? For a moment Mallory felt sick. The sounds of children's shrieks and laughter buzzed in her ears, the smell of frying potatoes made her stomach turn over.

She took a deep breath and on legs that felt too weak to support her, walked to Kent and Nick. No wonder the woman thought they were father and son. Anyone could see it. Even the way they stood was similar.

"Hey, Mom, did you hear?" Nick said as she came up to them. His signature grin lit up his face. "That lady thought I was Dr. Berger's kid. Funny, huh?"

"Uh-huh." *Hilarious.*

"We didn't tell her she made a mistake because she'd have been embarrassed, right, Dr. Berger?"

Kent's smile was a carbon copy of Nick's. "Right," he agreed and put a hand on the boy's shoulder. "You're a good kid, Nicholas."

"Yeah, my mom's done a great job with me. That's what everyone says."

"They're right." Kent turned to Mallory, admiration in his eyes.

"Thanks." She let out a shaky breath. Apparently Kent hadn't interpreted the woman's comment as anything more than the natural assumption that a man and boy standing together were father and son. She'd avoided disaster this time, she told herself, but if too many people noticed the resemblance and mentioned it, Kent really would catch on. Better not to get too involved with him. No more spontaneous meals at McDonald's. Nick could chat with him in the clinic, but that was all. She'd talk with Nick about that as soon as they got home.

She was silent in the car, pondering what to say to keep Nick from becoming too chummy with his doctor. This evening had given her a scare: her secret baby almost revealed against a backdrop of Happy Meals.

Lord, didn't she have enough to worry about? Nick's blood counts, his reactions to chemo and, looming ahead, the transplant. She'd forced herself not to think too much about that. It was too terrifying. She'd face the transplant when the time came.

From behind them came the sound of a soft snore. She turned to look at Nick. He was sprawled in the backseat with his arms splayed, his head against the cushion, eyes shut and mouth partially open. "He's exhausted," she murmured. "We shouldn't have stayed so long."

"Mallory, you can't lock him away from life. He has to be a normal kid, as normal as possible."

"I know," she sighed, "but I worry."

Kent glanced at her and gave her a half smile. "Sure you do, but you have to take time off, too, and take care of yourself."

Suddenly angry, Mallory glared at him. "That's what all doctors say, isn't it? Well, I can tell you it's impossible to take time off. What should I do—soak in a bubble bath? When you're a parent, wherever you go, the cancer goes with you." She bit her lip. She'd almost added, *How do you think you'd feel if you were Nick's father?*

"You're right." Kent lifted his hand from the steering wheel, moved it toward her as if to touch her, then stopped and returned it to the wheel. "I'm sorry," he murmured. "It's easy to speak in clichés when you're on the other side."

Mallory sighed. "And I'm sorry for jumping at you." She forced a smile. "So we're even."

Kent pulled up at her apartment.

"Nick, we're home," Mallory said.

He opened his eyes and stared at her sleepily, then yawned. "Okay."

Kent got out to walk them to the door. Mallory sent Nick inside, reminding him to brush his teeth before bed. "And—"

"I know," he said, "with the soft toothbrush." He grinned at Kent. "The leukemabrush, right?" Then he asked, "Aren't you coming in, Mom?"

"In a minute. I want to talk to Dr. Berger."

"'Kay. 'Night, Dr. Berger. I'll see you Thursday."

Mallory waited for Nick to shut the door, then squared her shoulders and turned to Kent. "About tonight—"

"He really is okay. Just a little tired."

She shook her head. "That's not what I wanted to talk about."

"What, then?"

She took a breath. "How often do you do this?"

"This?"

Was he being deliberately obtuse? "Eat at McDonald's."

He chuckled. "The last time was...oh, about ten years ago."

"Then why tonight? Surely you're not in the habit of going out for fast food with your patients."

His smile vanished. "No, I'm not."

"Then why Nick?"

Frowning, he hesitated a moment, then shook his head. "Damned if I know. Maybe because he's yours." He brushed his hand over her cheek, then as if he thought better of his gesture, he turned and walked quickly to his car.

Mallory stood still and watched him get into the car and pull out of the parking lot. Her cheek tingled where he'd touched her, even that faint contact setting off a wave of longing she thought had died long ago. It must have been simmering beneath the surface, needing only the brush of his fingers to come to life again.

She opened the door and went inside. This couldn't happen. Dammit, she wouldn't let it.

"That you, Mom?" Nick's sleepy voice called.

"Yes."

"I'm in bed."

She went to his room, sat on the edge of the bed and laid one hand on his cheek. She wished she could kiss him good night, but that wasn't allowed. Too likely to spread germs. She settled for blowing a kiss with her other hand.

Nick pretended to catch it. He yawned widely, then said, "Tonight was cool."

The perfect opening. "We need to talk about that."

His eyelids drooped. "'Kay," he muttered.

"I'm not sure it's a good idea to, um, be friends with Dr. Berger. To ask him out to dinner and, um, things like that."

His eyes opened. "Why?"

"Well, doctors have to make decisions about their patients, and being friends makes it harder."

"Adam Cage's family is friends with the Donnellys, and Dr. Donnelly is Adam's doctor."

"Yes," Mallory acknowledged, "but this is different. For instance, you needed that bone marrow aspiration. It hurt but it was important. Sometimes doctors have to make you feel bad to get you well, and doing that is hard if they're close friends with their patients."

Nick said nothing. He was clearly thinking this through.

"Do you understand?" Mallory asked.

"Yeah, kinda. You don't want me asking Dr. Berger to go somewhere with us."

"Exactly. I know you like him a lot, but…"

"That's okay, Mom. I get it. I can visit with him at the office."

Mallory squeezed his hand. "That lady at McDonald's was right. You are a sweetheart."

Nick made a gagging sound. "Sweetheart. Mom, puh-lease."

"Okay, tough guy. I won't say it again. I'll just think it," Mallory promised. "'Night."

"'Kay."

By the time she took the few steps to the door, she could hear by Nick's breathing that he'd fallen asleep. She sighed as she shut his door. Her son needed a father figure, especially now. Unfortunately, it appeared he'd chosen Kent.

Now what? It wasn't bedtime for her yet, but she was tired, stressed. Yet, unlike Nick, she couldn't instantly fall asleep. Why not take that bubble bath she'd mentioned to Kent? Her partner Lauri, who thought of everything, had slipped a jar of lavender bubble bath into Mallory's cosmetic case. She found it and poured a lavish amount into the tub and filled it to the top with warm water. She got out her favorite sleep shirt, hung it on the towel rack and shed her clothes, then lowered herself into the fragrant water and leaned back. Eyes shut, she let the bubbles tickle her shoulders. After a few minutes her stress level lowered. Yes, the leukemia was always with her, but the bath did help her relax.

But now her thoughts turned to Kent. She didn't want to remember the summer she'd been with him, but after spending this evening with him, she couldn't seem to help it. She ran her hand through the water, felt it lap against her breasts and imagined instead the soft caress of Kent's palm against her skin, the warmth of his mouth as he drew her nipple inside. When she opened her eyes, she saw that her nipples had tightened and the peaks extended above the water. She could almost feel the whisper of Kent's breath against her body, the tingle of anticipation inside her that signaled she wanted more of him, all of him.

"Go away, Kent," she murmured, then changed her mind. Nothing wrong with dreams, she told herself, as long as she stayed away from him in real life.

Kent poured himself a scotch, wandered into the great room of his house, glass in hand, and stared out the floor-to-ceiling windows with their view of the pool. What in hell had possessed him to accept Nick Brenner's invitation to join him and Mallory at McDonald's?

Okay, he had to admit he liked the kid. And he was fool enough to want to spend another evening with Mallory, even if it was for a dinner of burgers and fries. Something about her still tugged at him. Not just her looks, although she'd grown from a pretty girl to a beautiful woman. A strong woman, too. Life had dealt her a ton of blows—losing her husband and now facing her child's illness—but though there were shadows under her eyes, they still shone and her smile still beguiled him.

Damn, he shouldn't have touched her. The merest contact with her skin and he wanted more. Like an ex-drunk who tells himself he can get away with a taste of alcohol, he'd been sure he'd be satisfied with one light brush of his fingers over her cheek, but he'd been wrong. Now he craved her, wanted to run his hands and mouth over every inch of her…and have her touch him back.

She'd asked him about his marriage. Funny, he hadn't thought about Lisa in a long time, never looked deep inside himself to figure out why their marriage hadn't worked. If he wanted to be honest—something he hadn't been while the divorce was in progress—he'd admit he married Lisa on the rebound. He'd been looking for someone as different from Mallory as possible. Lisa was sophisticated, big-city; Mallory was the girl back home.

And suddenly he wondered if, right now, Mallory had a *guy* back home. Someone who'd be waiting when she got back to Valerosa, when Houston was only a memory. She'd had someone when he'd known her before. Dean Brenner had been waiting in the wings and as soon as Kent was out of sight—out of mind, too, he guessed—Dean had made his move. Or maybe Mallory had used *him* as bait to spur Dean on.

Kent lifted his glass and drank deeply, letting the liquor burn as it went down. The old attraction smoldered in him, the same as it had the first day he'd seen her, a cute lifeguard who gazed at him as if he were a hero. And though he warned himself not to forget she'd once played him for a fool, Kent knew he still wanted her.

Complicating everything was her kid. Tonight he'd broken one of his cardinal rules: never get involved with his patients.

That wasn't to say he didn't care about the children he treated. On the contrary, he cheered for them when they licked their illnesses, grieved with their families when they didn't make it. But he still kept his distance, maintained his objectivity.

But Nick was different. He was special. Kent took the last sip of scotch. Maybe he should turn the boy over to another doctor in the clinic. Then he'd be free to spend time with Nick and his mother outside the confines of the doctor/patient relationship.

But Nick needed him as a doctor. Kent was the pediatric AML specialist in the clinic in Houston.

Without arrogance, he knew he was the best doctor to treat the boy. If Nick had ALL, acute lymphocytic leukemia, the more common form of the disease in children, Kent knew he'd have no qualms about calling in another physician. But not in this case, not when the boy had a type of leukemia much rarer in youngsters.

So he'd continue on, but walk the line carefully between doctor…and friend.

The following week, Nick bounded out of the examining room with eyes shining. "Guess what, Mom," he whispered to Mallory as they left the clinic. "I didn't ask Dr. Berger to go out with us. *He* did the asking. And oh, yeah, he told me to see what you thought."

"He did?" Whatever Kent had suggested, Mallory was sure it wasn't a good idea. Her heart sank. In her mind, she glared fiercely at Kent. *Damn him.* "What did he say?"

"Wait till you hear, Mom. You're not gonna believe this. He has a friend in the Astros organization." Nick's smile widened. "He's gonna get us tickets to a baseball game."

Chapter Six

Mallory stared at her son as they crossed the parking lot. For the moment she was speechless, trying to figure out who Kent's invitation included. "Us" as in her and Nick? Offering the two of them tickets would be a generous gesture, but somehow she didn't think that was what Kent had in mind. Did "us" mean Nick and Kent? The thought of Kent spending time alone with her son—*his* son—made her extremely nervous. Or did "us" mean all three of them? Another friendly evening. She wasn't sure she could handle this much chumminess with Kent. Across the desk in his medical office was one thing, but sitting next to him for a whole evening, hearing the deep cadence of his voice, literally rubbing shoulders with him, that was something else. Something she'd be smart to avoid.

"Mom, you haven't said a word," Nick said. "Are you stunned?" He grinned. "That was one of our vocabulary words this year. It means frozen or shocked. I remembered."

"I guess I am a little stunned, and congratulations on remembering the word."

"Well, isn't Dr. Berger's idea great?"

"Great." Sighing, she opened the car door and got in. Nick walked to the passenger door and slid in beside her. "Buckle your seat belt," she ordered.

Her son rolled his eyes. "Don't I always? Come on, Mom. Isn't this the most awesome news?"

Mallory forced a smile. "Sure is." She glanced at Nick. "You didn't, like, give Dr. Berger a little nudge in that direction, did you?"

He stared at her blankly. "Nudge?"

"Nudge—a gentle shove. New vocabulary word." Inside the steamy car she started the engine, turned the air conditioner on high and wiped the perspiration off her forehead. Houston humidity was unbearable. How did these people make it through a summer? She backed out of the parking space as she waited for Nick's answer.

"No, ma'am." Nick's smile was as innocent as a baby's. "'Course he knows I love baseball…."

"And the Astros."

"Yeah."

"Well, it was very nice of him. Did he, uh, say when you two would be going?"

"Not us two. All three of us. Mom, you know you like baseball, too. And this is *major league.*"

She chuckled in spite of herself. "Right. So when's the big day?"

"Night," Nick corrected. "He said we'd go to an evening game."

They didn't talk the rest of the short drive home. While Nick basked in the anticipation of the ball game, Mallory's mind whirled in confusion. One minute she was grateful to Kent for his kindness to Nick; the next, she was annoyed with him for increasing their social contact. Wasn't he inadvertently setting Nick up for a fall? He was becoming important to Nick, and her son would be that much more dejected when they returned to Valerosa and his association with Kent was over.

Why was Kent doing this? she asked herself as she pulled into the driveway of their apartment building. Suspicion of his motives nagged at her. The memory of his brief touch haunted her, the longing to be with him again pulled at her.

Nick smiled through dinner and chattered excitedly about the Astros' lineup, their schedule, their win-loss record. As soon as dinner was over, Mallory sent him to bed. He needed to be up early. He would start another round of chemo tomorrow. And she needed some quiet time to think about how she was going to handle the evening out with Kent.

She was afraid Nick was too revved up to sleep, but he nodded off within a few minutes, and she got out her journal. Maybe writing about her feelings would help her sort through them.

She paged back through the entries for the last week. *Oh, good grief, no,* she thought as she read. Even before their dinner at McDonald's, Kent's name appeared on almost every page, and since their evening together, almost every paragraph. Her feelings about him as a doctor—*I trust him with Nick's life*—and as a man—*I'd forgotten how his smile makes me feel—warm and shivery at the same time*. Heavens, she sounded like a teenager again.

She picked up her pen and began to write. By the time she'd covered three pages with script, her feelings for Kent were no clearer, but she'd come to a decision: she would not deny Nick the opportunity to see the Astros play. *Major league*. She hoped an Astros player would hit one out of the park. That would make Nick's evening unforgettable. Imagining Nick's delight, she smiled and got up to lock the journal in her suitcase.

Yawning, she rubbed her eyes. Clinic days were always tiring. Might as well get to bed. She undressed, took off her makeup and, sitting on the side of her bed, whispered her nightly prayer for Nick's recovery. "May he be blessed with a complete healing in his spirit and in his body. Amen."

She lay down, shut her eyes and drifted off....

A shriek woke her.

"Mom! Mommy!"

Nick! Terrified, she jumped out of bed, glancing at the alarm clock on her nightstand. Two-thirty. "I'm coming," she called and raced into his room.

There was enough light from the hallway to illuminate his face. He was sitting up in bed, his eyes wide with fear, his mouth slack.

She would not let him see how frightened she was. She kept her voice low, even. "What's wrong, hon?"

"I had to go to the bathroom. I rolled over, and I felt something on me. On my face."

Mallory let out a breath. She'd been ready for

anything—fever, nausea—and it was nothing. "Probably a bug," she said. "A harmless one, I imagine." She'd ask the apartment manager to call an exterminator in the morning.

"No!" Nick shouted. "It's still there. It's all over me. Look."

"Okay." She reached behind her and flipped the light switch. Nick's face and chest were covered with tufts of hair. More clumps of hair littered the pillow. Mallory refused to allow herself to react. "Honey, it's not a bug. It's…it's your hair. The chemo's made it fall out."

"No." He rubbed his head, stared down at his hand. Bits of hair clung to his fingers. *"No,"* he shouted.

"Nicky, you've seen lots of kids whose hair has fallen out."

"Not mine."

Mallory sat down beside him, tried to put her arms around him, but he shoved her away. "I'm gonna be bald. You hear that, Mom? Bald." His small fists clenched. "I want to see."

He pushed past her and lunged toward the bathroom. Mallory followed, watched as he turned on the light and stared into the mirror at the sparse hair still covering his head. "Oh, gross, Mom. Gross."

Seeing him like this hurt her, too. Nick's beautiful hair, thick and curly, the same chestnut-brown as Kent's, falling out as he swiped a hand over his head. But she swallowed the lump in her throat and said, "We'll get your head shaved in the morning. And we'll buy you an Astros cap."

Despite his emotional outburst, Nick had the presence of mind to scowl at her. His gaze stayed trained on the mirror. Suddenly he turned on her, tears welling in his eyes. "Around here it's okay to be bald, but what about when I get home? What'll happen when I go to school? Kids'll think I'm a freak."

What could she say? "Oh, honey." Her heart hurt for him. She gathered him into her arms and held him tight as his tears soaked her nightgown.

Suddenly he pulled away. "I wanna talk to Dr. Berger."

Startled, Mallory stared at him. "Nick, it's the middle of the night."

"Doctors work in the middle of the night. Jeremy's mom called Dr. Berger at 4:00 a.m."

"Jeremy was running a fever. He was sick."

"I got *leukemia*. That's 'sick,' isn't it?" Nick folded his arms across his chest and glared at her.

She wasn't sure why, but something in his stubborn stance reminded her of Kent. "Not sick in the same way," she said in as reasonable a tone as she could muster. "You can talk to Dr. Berger in the morning. We'll call the clinic."

Nick seemed to weigh this, then gave in with a not-too-graceful scowl. "Soon's I get up," he muttered.

"Just as soon," she echoed, hating that he was becoming so attached to Kent. Would she feel that way if he had a different doctor and had asked to call? She wasn't sure. All she knew, as she led him back to bed, was that being the mother of a sick child was hard enough without the added pressure of having his as-yet-unsuspecting father as his doctor.

She sat by Nick's bed until he fell back to sleep, praying this time that she would keep her sanity through this ordeal.

In the morning she woke at six-thirty to find Nick standing by her bed. Her throat caught. He'd lost more hair during the night. Brown strands clung to his pajama top. "Call," he demanded.

She went out to the kitchen and dialed Kent's answering service. In minutes the phone rang. Nick picked it up and gestured for her to leave the room.

Mallory went back in her bedroom and shut the door. In the early morning quiet she could hear the murmur of Nick's voice. She wondered what he said to Kent, what Kent answered, but she promised herself she wouldn't ask. When Nick opened her door a few minutes later, she said, "Okay?"

His face expressionless, he nodded. "Okay."

"I'll call the barber shop at the hospital later and make an appointment," Mallory said.

"Yeah."

In the afternoon after Nick's chemo and the visit to the hospital barber shop she drove to nearby Rice Village, a multiblock complex of stores and restaurants. Finding a parking place wasn't easy in this popular shopping area, but Mallory saw a car pulling out of a spot only a block from the sporting goods store. She beat a car coming from the opposite direction and swerved into the space.

"Come on," she said opening her door.

Nick didn't move. "The store's way down the block."

"I know. There weren't any parking spaces way down the block."

He stuck out his lower lip. "You go."

"Honey, it's hot in the car."

Nick glowered at her. "I know. I'm not going."

He was embarrassed at his baldness. She wouldn't push. "Okay, I'll be right back."

The store carried dozens of home team caps along with those of other major league teams. Mallory picked up a red Astros cap in a small size, then another. Nick's head size would be smaller now without his thick crop of hair. She frowned at the caps, unsure which would fit. Damn, cancer invaded every corner of your life. "This one," she muttered, took the cap to the counter and hurried back to the car.

She could see him sitting in the front seat, this little stranger with a bald head. She opened the door and saw that his head was shiny with sweat. Somehow that made her want to cry, but she pasted on a smile and handed him the cap. He turned it from side to side, examining it, then put it on without comment.

After the emotional day Mallory wasn't prepared for Catherine Garland's voice on the answering machine. "Mrs. Brenner, please call the clinic."

Why? With shaking fingers, Mallory punched in the number. She had to wait several minutes before Catherine came on the line. "What is it?" she asked.

"No problems with Nick," Catherine said, "but I wanted you to know we've made an appointment for you on Monday at eleven-thirty with Dr. McNeece. He's the transplant specialist."

Mallory sat down. "Trans…isn't it too early for that?"

"Not really. Since Nick has no siblings who could donate, you'll need time to find a donor."

"Oh," she murmured. She'd known this was coming, but not so soon. She hadn't prepared.

Suddenly she completely understood Nick's feelings and his need for Kent last night. She swallowed. "May I please speak to Dr. Berger?"

Chapter Seven

Mallory's hands trembled as she waited for Kent to pick up the phone.

"Yes, Mallory," he said. His calm voice dispelled some of her tension…but not all.

"I understand we're to see the, uh, transplant doctor next week." Her muscles tightened again. Saying the word "transplant" made her feel queasy.

"That's right."

"I'd like to ask you a few questions." A lie. She'd like him to tell her there was no need to think about a transplant, that Nick would get well without it.

"Dr. McNeese will explain ev—" he began, then stopped. "You're scared."

"A little." Another lie. She was terrified, and her voice must be giving her away.

"I'll be finished seeing patients in about an hour," he said. "Then I have to make rounds…. No, I'll do that later. Can you leave Nick with one of the other families and come by the office?"

She seized on his offer like a lifeline. "Yes. Thank you." Weak with relief, she hung up and sank into a chair, then shook her head disgustedly. Good grief, she was loath to have Nick become dependent on Kent and now here she was, doing the same thing herself.

She found her phone list and called Tamara Spellman. "Could you do me a favor and keep Nick for an hour or so? I have an appointment with Dr. Berger."

"Is something wrong?" Tamara asked.

"No, I just have some questions."

"Transplant coming up," Tamara guessed.

"Yeah."

"Tough to think about," Tamara said, empathizing in the way only another parent of a kid with cancer could. "Sure, bring Nick over. He and Jeremy can play with their Game Boys. I don't know who invented those things, but when I find out, I'm remembering him in my will."

"Me, too," Mallory agreed. "Thanks."

She left Nick at Jeremy's and headed for the clinic. While she was there, she'd talk to Kent about the baseball tickets. Nick was counting on them. She wanted Kent to reassure her that he wouldn't be disappointed.

When she got to the office and signed in, only one youngster, a small, pale girl with a bandanna tied around her head, was left in the usually crowded and noisy waiting room. The little girl's mother sat disinterestedly thumbing through a dog-eared copy of *People.* She wore the resigned look of a woman for whom waiting had become a way of life. Mallory flashed her an understanding smile, took a seat and picked up another outdated magazine. When the nurse called the child's name, she and her mother plodded through the door, leaving behind them mingled echoes of hope and despair.

Mallory laid her magazine down and waited. Fifteen minutes passed, then the window opened and Cory, the receptionist, her voice still impressively cheerful for the end of the day, called Mallory in and waved her down the hall. "You can go on in the office. The doctor will be right there," she instructed.

As Mallory headed toward Kent's office, she heard behind her the sounds of the receptionist and insurance clerks gathering their personal things and chatting about their plans for the evening. It seemed a long time since she'd been that carefree. She pushed open the door to Kent's spacious office, took a chair and glanced around. She'd been here before but hadn't really paid much attention to the surroundings. Thick carpeting and expensive furnishings proclaimed Kent's status in the medical world. Diplomas and certificates, expensively framed, covered one wall next to a bookcase filled with medical books and journals.

Two watercolors of sailboats adorned another wall. She imagined Kent sailing, face turned toward the sun, the wind mussing his hair. Did he enjoy sailing, or had he just liked the pictures? Mallory wondered. She knew little about the hobbies and interests he might have developed over the years. Not that she should care. His life beyond the clinic and hospital was none of her business. Yet she found herself staring at the paintings, then at a group of nature photographs on the opposite wall. Had he taken them or bought them somewhere? Were the settings important to him?

To distract herself from her curiosity about Kent and her worries over the transplant, she walked to the window. On the sill was a bright yellow "sunflower" constructed of small plastic blocks. Nick had asked Kent about it one day and he'd said it was a gift from a former patient and his father to make up for the lack of real plants. Mallory smiled at the meticulous detail of the plant, down to one tiny yellowed "leaf."

When she'd gone to the gift shop Nick's first day in the hospital, she'd wondered why there was no florist, but she'd soon learned that plants and flowers were forbidden to leukemia patients, along with fresh fruits and vegetables. She'd sighed at the lack of growing things; Nick had applauded the vegetable taboo. "No more broccoli. No more cauliflower," he crowed, pumping his fists and chanting like a high-school cheerleader.

Mallory studied the plant's plastic leaves. To be more realistic, they should be spaced just a little farther apart. She fingered one, itching to move it—

She heard the door open, jumped and turned as Kent came into the office. "Is the plant doctor making a house call?" he inquired.

"You caught me," she admitted.

He came to stand beside her. "You must miss having plants around."

She shrugged. "It's a small sacrifice."

"You'll have them back eventually," he said.

Mallory's eyes filled suddenly, as they often did nowadays. "Will I?"

"You know I can't give you any guarantees, but the chances are good."

He'd probably said this to dozens of parents, hundreds she supposed, as he put a hand on her back and urged her to return to her chair. His touch was impersonal and she imagined he'd done *that* hundreds of times, too. Yet she longed to lean into his hand, to lean into *him*. She wanted comfort, reassurance. She wanted oblivion. Foolish.

She sat down, and he took the seat across the desk, pushed some pink message slips aside and leaned forward. "The chances improve with a transplant," he said.

She clasped her hands in her lap. "Enough to risk it?"

"Absolutely."

Her hands tightened until the fingers ached. "I've read about the transplant process. First you kill off all his blood cells. He won't have an immune system." She couldn't stem the flow of words, the icy fear in her voice. "There won't be any white cells left to protect him. What if the transplant doesn't work? Then what?"

"Then we'll try again."

"You make it sound easy," she muttered.

"I'm sorry if I do," Kent said softly. "It's never easy. And I told you in the beginning, I won't lie to you. The chances of a good match would be better with a sibling."

Mallory stared down at her hands. Even if she and Dean had had children together, Nick would only have a half sibling. But of course she couldn't tell Kent that.

She and Dean had tried to have children and had even visited a fertility clinic in Dallas. They'd learned that Dean's sperm count was low, and after they'd discussed their options, he'd said in a voice filled with emotion that Nick was enough for him. He'd loved Nick unequivocally.

She thought of a picture she kept on her desk at the florist shop: the three of them at the park on the way to a family picnic, Dean with Nick hoisted on his shoulder and a big grin on his face. He'd been a great dad. He'd promised her when he asked her to marry him that he'd raise Nick as his own. She'd worried about that as her pregnancy advanced and they were living in El Paso, where Dean attended college. On nights when he was at the library and she was alone, she'd stare out the window at the sparse desert and the mountains, wondering how he'd feel when he was actually faced with another man's child. But when Nick was born and she saw the look of awe and love on Dean's face, she knew that marrying him had been the right thing to do, and she'd never regretted it.

She looked up to find Kent watching her. "What?" she asked.

"You should be tested," he said. "So should your parents and Dean's. The chances for a match are much lower with parents or grandparents. Still, you need to be screened."

"Yes, okay." Along with her own parents, she would ask the Brenners. They would think it strange if she didn't.

"You told me once your great-grandparents were immigrants. Where did they come from?" Kent asked.

"Ukraine. Why?"

"If you have to find a donor through the registry, you'll need to restrict the search for Jews of Eastern European extraction."

After a moment she realized the implications. "A smaller donor pool," she murmured.

"Or you can think more optimistically. In that group you'll have a better chance for a match."

For a moment they were both silent, then Mallory spoke, her tone pleading. "Why do we have to do this? Aren't there other options?"

He gazed at her steadily. "As of today, July seventh, no."

Her heart fell. She'd known he'd say that, but stubbornly, she clung to a shred of hope. "Can't we wait for the chemo to work?" she asked. "Isn't that the reason you give it? To cure the leukemia."

"He's getting it to put him in remission. Transplants are most successful if they're done during the first remission."

"*First.* That means it may not last and he may relapse." Logically, she knew this, but she couldn't seem to face the possibility. Now she had to. "We could be putting him through all this for nothing," she said bitterly.

"We're putting him through this to get him ready for the best chance he has for a cure," Kent corrected in a firm voice.

Mallory shut her eyes, but she couldn't shut out the truth of Kent's words. "You're right, of course," she sighed. "I haven't let myself think far enough ahead to get to the transplant." She wanted to drop her head into her hands and cry out all her pain and fear. Instead, she stood and extended a hand across the desk. "I've taken a lot of your time. Thanks for letting me come in."

Kent took her hand and held it tightly for a moment. "I'm always here for…" He paused. "For parents."

"Thanks." She turned away. "I'll let myself out."

As she shut the door, she thought she heard him call her name, but she hurried down the hall. She didn't want him to see the tears that were pooling over now. She walked numbly across the parking lot toward her car.

Kent stood at the window and watched her go. When she got into the car, he saw her swipe a hand across her cheek. She'd been crying.

He'd started to call her back when she left his office, but she hadn't heard and he'd let her go. When she'd thanked him and he'd told her he was here for parents, he'd almost said, "I'm here for *you,*" then he'd caught himself. Too personal.

He wanted to be there for Mallory, to pull her into his arms and tell her Nick was going to be fine, but even though he fully believed that, he couldn't make an unequivocal statement. Not even the best doctor could predict the future. No physician could play God. There was always that chance that something would go wrong.

He knew it was tough for parents to live with that. Sometimes the uncertainty split families apart. He wondered if Dean had lived, whether he'd have been the rock that Mallory needed. Kent wished he could play that role, but he could only be the supportive doctor, not the caring man. But God help him, he wanted to be both.

In the parking lot, Mallory put the car in Drive. She didn't want to go home and she knew an extra half hour or so wouldn't matter to Tamara, so she went for a ride, driving aimlessly through neighborhoods near the medical center. She passed comfortable houses, green lawns, bicycles and skateboards. Nice, ordinary lives. From the outside, anyway.

She slowed as she came to a park where youngsters were milling around, obviously getting ready for a

Little League game. Younger children and parents filled the bleachers.

A lump clogged Mallory's throat. How many summers had she been part of the Little League scene? In her mind's eye, she could see Nick in his natty baseball uniform, see herself clad in T-shirt and cutoffs. The scorching sunlight would have been gone by game time but the night air would still be heavy with heat. She could see the tall poles around the ball diamond with their big bulbs haloed by light and clouds of moths swarming around them. She could smell grass and popcorn, hear her own voice yelling encouragement to Nick as he chased a ball or ran the bases.

She'd enjoyed those carefree nights, but had she cherished each one, understood how precious those hours were? Did anyone? She guessed no one realized what they had until it was snatched away. Brushing aside the tears that slid down her cheeks, she drove on.

As she made her way back to the apartment, she noticed a plant nursery. She thought of Kent's sunflower and smiled, thinking how on target he'd been when he said she must miss plants.

Impulsively, she pulled into a parking space and went into the nursery. She couldn't have plants inside, but why not outside? She'd make a garden. There was a perfect spot behind the apartment house. All she needed were tools, some rose bushes and elbow grease. Twenty minutes later she had everything she needed.

It wasn't until she pulled into her carport that she realized she'd forgotten to ask Kent about the Astros tickets.

* * *

The garden was the best therapy Mallory could have thought of. She'd bought roses in every hue: Freedom in yellow, Mountbatten in gold with pink rims, Bonica in pink and every shade of red she could find from crimson to vermillion. She got up early every morning to work in the garden, leaving Nick with instructions to knock on the window that looked out on the flower bed if he needed anything. One morning he did, scaring her to death, but he only grinned and gestured something she couldn't understand. She raced around to the front and went inside. "What?" she panted.

"I want a rose bush," he said.

"Nick, you know you can't work in the garden." When he was small, he'd loved to join her as she gardened. He'd make mud pies, watch for bugs, beg for a handful of seeds to plant.

"You can work for me," he said. "I want my own bush."

"Okay. Come back to the window and show me which one. Then you can make a little sign and we'll put it by your bush." He chose Crimson Glory and stood at the window gesturing to her until she had the bush exactly where he wanted it. Mallory smiled to herself. Maybe Nick would grow up to be a landscape architect. When she finished planting to his satisfaction, he went to work on the sign and soon it was in place.

As the days passed, other parents came out to work alongside Mallory, and their children selected bushes, too. The rose garden became a community project.

Mallory was pleased but sometimes she preferred the early hour when she worked alone. She'd always loved working with the soil.

She'd been gardening the day Nick was conceived, weeding her mother's rose bed on a sweltering summer afternoon, when Kent drove up. She swiped the back of her hand across her sweaty face as he strolled toward her.

"Hi," he said and knelt beside her. "I thought I'd pick up some barbecue and we could have a picnic supper at Bear Creek Park."

"Okay. What time?"

"Seven-thirty. You have mud on your cheek," he murmured and wiped it gently with his thumb. Just that touch and the look in his eyes, hot and hungry, made her heart pound and her lips part.

"I want to kiss you," he told her. "Right here in the front yard, with your mother watching from behind the curtains."

She grinned. "No one's home."

"The neighbors are," he said, glancing at the car parked in the next driveway.

"Kiss me anyway," she said, a challenge in her voice.

"All right." He cupped her chin, drew her closer, and covered her lips with his. "How was that?"

"Not enough."

"We'll remedy that tonight." He'd dropped another kiss on her nose, stood, and headed for his car.

She would always remember those moments—the heat of the sun, the smell of roses and freshly turned earth, the laughter in his eyes as he kissed her. She would never forget that afternoon. The day her life changed forever.

As the July temperature increased and the humidity along with it, Mallory's patience grew thin. She was less tolerant of Nick's occasional surliness as she worried about the results of the blood tests her family had taken. Why did the matching take so long? Although other parents assured her this was perfectly normal, she found herself waking at night and unable to fall back to sleep.

After a few days, Nick's excitement over the Astros tickets wore off and changed to frustration. "When is Dr. Berger going to get the tickets?" he whined. Before she could answer, he added, "And, no, I didn't pester him about them."

"You just pester me," Mallory muttered, but she, too, was becoming annoyed. Not just with Nick's whining but with Kent, too. Who knew better than she that Dr. Berger, the medical icon, didn't always keep his word? He'd once told Mallory he loved her, that he wanted a future with her. And then he'd disappeared.

She remembered how elated Kent had been when his mentor, Dr. Charles Wilson, had invited him to accompany him to a medical conference in Milan. He'd be back soon, he promised Mallory. When the conference was over, he'd come straight to Valerosa.

"I love you," he'd said. "Only you." And Mallory had believed him.

But he'd never come back. Never even called.

If he'd reneged on something that important, she wasn't surprised he'd forgotten the baseball tickets. Well, she'd just see about that. Dammit, he wasn't getting away with it.

Chapter Eight

When they arrived at the clinic that afternoon, Mallory rang the bell and waited impatiently at the window until Cory opened it. "I'd like to speak with Dr. Berger for a few minutes before he sees Nick."

Beside her, Nick started. "Why, Mom?" he asked.

When she turned, Mallory saw the apprehension in his eyes. Darn, she should have expected that and made arrangements to see Kent while Nick was getting blood drawn. She took his arm and drew him toward a chair, then sat beside him. "It's nothing. I just want to ask him something."

He moved closer. "Am I getting sicker?"

Damn. *Dammit.* She shouldn't have been so impulsive. "Of course not. You don't feel sick, do you?" When he shook his head but still looked scared, she knew she had to tell him the truth. "I wanted to ask him about the Astros tickets." She saw her son's look of relief and mentally kicked herself for frightening him.

"What are you gonna ask him about the tickets?" Nick said.

She sighed. "When he's getting them." Meaning *if* he's getting them.

Nick gave her a sly smile. "So *you're* going to pester him? I thought you said that was impolite."

Had she thought Nick would become a landscape architect? This child was going to grow up to be a lawyer. "I'm going to pester him in a grown-up way."

"Can I come with you?"

"No."

"Why not?"

"Because I said so." Before he could say another word, she said sternly, "Nick, *no*." She dumped a copy of *Sports Illustrated for Kids* in his lap.

He said nothing, only frowned at her over the top of the magazine. But when Catherine Garland opened the door and called her name, she heard him whisper, "You go, Mom."

She certainly intended to.

Catherine tapped on Kent's door, opened it and stood aside. He was at his desk. "Hey, Ni—" he began. "Mallory?"

As soon as the door shut behind her, she marched over to the desk and stood with her hands on her hips. All her training in "grown-up" politeness deserted her. "I want to talk to you," she snapped.

"I can see that," Kent said mildly. "Sit down."

She shook her head, leaned her hands on the desk and

stared him straight in the eyes. "Nick is upset, and dammit, so am I. You made promises to him."

"I—" he began.

But, temper steaming, Mallory didn't stop. "You should know you can't do that to a kid and not follow through. Not to a well kid but especially not to a sick one."

When she paused for breath, he opened his desk drawer. "Promises," he said. "You mean about these?" He took out an envelope, held it open and three tickets fluttered to the desk.

Deflated and embarrassed, Mallory sank into a chair. "Oh," she muttered. "I'm…uh, sorry."

A smile playing on his lips, he said, "That's quite all right, Mom. I'm sure you were both getting impatient, but I had to wait to get these until Nick was in remission."

For a moment, the words didn't register. When they did, she gasped. "Remission. He's in remission? Oh, dear God!" Tears overflowed. Happy ones at last. She pulled a tissue from her purse and dabbed at her eyes. "Why didn't you tell me?"

He chuckled. "I just did. The lab reports came in this morning, and the tickets were sent over an hour later."

"Oh, my gosh, I have to call my family," she said, no longer trying to stem her tears. She put her hands back on the desk and leaned toward Kent. "Thank you."

"For the tickets, you're welcome." He smiled gently. "For the remission? You're a rabbi's daughter. You know I didn't do that by myself."

"You're right." She smiled at him. "But thanks anyway."

"Why don't you go get Nick and we'll talk about his remission and the ball game?"

Drying her tears, Mallory hurried back to the waiting room. She waved to Nick. "Come on in."

Nick's eyes zeroed in on her still damp cheeks. "Is…is something wrong?"

"No, it's good news. Really good," she whispered as she grasped his arm and hurried him down the hall.

In the office, Kent smiled broadly at Nick, who still seemed apprehensive. "Well, pal, great news. You're in remission." When Nick gave him a puzzled look, Kent explained, "Those evil blasts are gone."

"No kidding? We've defeated them?"

"Killed them off," Kent agreed.

"Wow! Does that mean I can—"

"Go to an Astros game now? Sure does."

"Oh, geez. Awesome. Mom, did you hear that?"

Mallory laughed. "I did."

Nick turned to Kent. "Guess that's why she's crying. Girls do that," he added, man to man.

Kent laughed. "Yeah, but we like them anyway." His eyes caught Malloy's and lingered, his gaze caressing.

Her skin heated, tingled, as it had years ago whenever he would catch her eye across the pool. She forced her gaze away and turned to Nick. "Did you say thank you?" she asked in a stage whisper.

"Thanks, Dr. Berger. About the game—when is it and who're they playing?"

"Next Wednesday. The Cardinals. It's going to be crowded, so we'll go early and stay until the stadium clears out."

At the mention of crowds, Mallory asked, "Should Nick wear a mask?"

"Aw, Mom," her son mumbled.

"The answer is yes," Kent said, then turned to Nick. "Germs are tricky characters. We're not going to take any chances."

"Okay."

"Now you need to go into the exam room and let the lab folks draw some blood."

"Shoot, I thought remission meant that'd be over," Nick muttered, but he smiled as he left the room.

Mallory got up to follow, but Kent said, "Stay a minute."

She sat down again and he asked, "How are you holding up?"

"Up and down, but over all pretty well," she answered honestly. "Wishing it didn't take so long to find out if there's a match for Nick, but I'm keeping busy so that helps."

"I've heard about your garden."

Something in his voice, in his eyes, made her wonder if he, too, remembered that long-ago day among the roses. She met his eyes, and for a moment the old magic between them seemed to sizzle in the air. But that was crazy. They weren't the same two people anymore, hadn't been for years.

Don't let it happen all over again, she ordered herself, knowing something *was* happening, no matter how firmly she lectured herself. She cleared her throat. "Who told you about the garden?"

"My newest patient's mom."

"Karen LeMay." Relieved to have something to distract her, Mallory said, "Did you know her son Steven's taught the other kids to play poker? They're really hooked, even little Becky Peterson. They play every evening. For pennies."

Kent chuckled. "How's Nick doing?"

"He's ahead about twelve cents. The parents are thinking of forming a poker club, too. Higher stakes, of course. Maybe nickels."

"If you need any pointers, let me know."

There it was again, that little zing of electricity that seemed to shoot across his desk. "Are you a poker player?"

"Not a very good one. I play with a group of other docs who get together once a month. I played a lot in medical school though."

She hadn't known that, hadn't known a lot of things about him, although at the time they were together, she thought she knew everything. Well, she didn't want to know too much, not now. Didn't want to picture Kent relaxed, sitting at the card table with a bunch of guys, with his shirtsleeves rolled up to the elbows, forearms bare, maybe a beer in his hand.

Easing out of her chair, she said, "Thank you again for the tickets. I guess we'll see you next Wednesday."

"The game starts at seven. I'll pick you up at quarter to five. That'll be time enough to avoid the rush." He grinned. "These tickets come with a reserved parking space."

Mallory grinned back. "Awesome."

She and Nick spent a good deal of time the next few days discussing the issue of the mask. "I hate it," Nick said as he undressed one evening. He kicked his sneaker across the bathroom.

"You don't have to like it, but you have to wear it," Mallory said, staring pointedly at the shoe.

Scowling, Nick picked it up and set it beside its mate. "I know," he groused. "It's okay around the hospital, but somewhere else... People will stare at me." He yanked off his T-shirt. "Those masks make you look like a duck. They're weird."

Mallory understood his feelings. The yellow duck-billed masks did indeed draw attention. She sighed, then brightened. "Well, if people are going to stare at you and you're going to look weird, why not go all the way? Look *really* weird."

Nick frowned. "How much weirder could I look?"

"Let's decorate a mask and we'll see."

He thought for a moment, then a slow smile spread across his face. "We can do it with Astros stickers."

"Yeah."

"And a slogan: Duck, you Cardinals. The Astros are coming."

"Now you're cooking," Mallory said. Nick looked befuddled, and she added, "It's an idiom. Means you're moving along, doing great."

When Wednesday afternoon finally arrived, Nick was ready. He wore his Astros cap and a Clay Parker jersey, with his decorated mask folded in the pocket. He danced back and forth to the window to look for Kent's car, checked his watch and generally drove Mallory insane. But she couldn't fault him. She was pretty excited herself.

When the doorbell rang at precisely 4:45 p.m., Nick scurried to answer. He flung the door open. "Hi, Doctor Berger," he cried, and there was Kent wearing an Astros T-shirt and cap of his own.

Weren't they a pair, Mallory thought, as they turned to watch her cross to the door. She felt a bittersweet pang. Wouldn't Dean be proud to know what a fine son he'd raised?

And wouldn't Kent, if he knew what a great kid he'd sired? When she told him—someday—she hoped he'd remember this outing with pleasure.

"Let's get moving," Kent said, and they piled into the Jaguar for the ride downtown. From the backseat, Nick kept up a constant chatter.

Soon Minute Maid Park loomed up before them, looking for all the world as if it had been transplanted from Disney World, with its orangy-red brick and turquoise steel girders.

They drove right up to the valet parking entrance and left the car with a young man who looked not much older than Nick. This was Mallory's first experience with valet parking. Valerosa didn't offer such amenities. She heard the young man gun the motor as he drove off and hoped the car would return unscathed. Kent seemed unconcerned.

As they walked toward the entrance, Nick said, "Wow, look at those baseballs."

Mallory saw them, lined up along the sidewalk, each big enough to provide an uncomfortable looking seat for a full-grown man. "Maybe when we get inside, we can buy a postcard with a picture of them," she said.

"No problem. I brought my camera," Kent said. "The two of you have a seat."

Mallory and Nick climbed onto a giant ball, posed and mugged for the camera.

"Mask on now," Kent said. Nick drew it out of his

pocket with a flourish and Kent, appropriately impressed, insisted on snapping a picture of "the masked Astro fan." Then they walked up the ramp and entered the ballpark.

More Fantasyland. Most of the souvenir shops and concessions that ringed the walkway were still closed, but a few were open and getting ready for business. The odors of popcorn and beer wafted toward them through the air. The *cool* air. Another fantasy come true for a small-town girl, Mallory thought. A baseball game in midsummer in an air-conditioned stadium. Double wow!

As they walked, Nick gave a little skip and squeezed Mallory's hand. "Is this amazing, or what?" he whispered.

Mallory nodded. She felt like skipping herself. Her thoughts echoed Nick's. *Major league!*

They bought programs and found their box, behind home plate. The field was Ireland-green, the scoreboard appropriately flamboyant and the little train that Kent explained would chug back and forth whenever an Astro hit a home run was an eye-catcher. And when game time approached and they rose for the national anthem sung by a local favorite, Mallory watched Nick remove his cap without complaint. His bald head clearly didn't concern him as he laid his hand over his heart and faced the flag. Seeing him, her own heart filled to overflowing.

And then there was the game itself, a tight one, with the lead seesawing back and forth. It was almost too much to take in—the Astros in their bright red jerseys, the Cards in gray, the crack of the bat hitting a ball, the chug of the little train when Jeff Barrick, one of Nick's favorite Astros, hit a homer into far right field, the shouts and cheers, the lights, the music.

Kent took pictures left and right. From their seats, they could just see into the Astros' dugout, see one of the rookie outfielders chomping on his gum and blowing huge bubbles. The camera clicked. Two players lounged against the outer wall, chatting with one another. Another click.

"Mom, that's Pete Maloney." Nick's excited voice came out in a squeak.

"Who?"

"Puh-lease, Mom. He's the—"

"The closer," she said in unison with him, then laughed. "Gotcha."

"She knows a lot…for a girl," Kent said, and winked at her, setting her heart pounding foolishly. He looked so appealing, with a light stubble on his cheeks and his eyes teasing. She wished they were a real family and Kent could reach over and squeeze her hand. Not with a sexy touch but an intimate one, the way a man touched the wife who'd shared his life for many years.

During the game she watched Kent and Nick, heads together, discussing pitching strategy when the Cardinals' clean-up batter, Rafe Mendoza, came up, with one out and two on base. For a moment, she let herself imagine what might have been. Kent and Nick, father and son; Kent and herself, husband and wife. Why had everything gone wrong for them?

Was there a chance for them now? Crazy thought, with her secret, literally, between them. Longing filled her for what could never be, and she sighed.

Kent turned to her. "Something wrong?"

"Nothing." *Nothing that can be easily fixed.*

"Sure?"

She nodded, and he turned back to the game while Mallory continued to watch him. Watch and wish.

When the game was over, with the Astros winning by two, they watched the stadium empty out and then Kent said, "I have a surprise."

"Another surprise?" Mallory asked, thinking he'd done enough. This had been one of the most memorable days of her son's life.

Kent's eyes crinkled. "A special one." He stood and signaled an usher, who started down the stairs toward them. "Good thing you wore that jersey, pal," he said to Nick. "We're going to meet Clay Parker."

For a moment Nick said nothing, only stared, wide-eyed and speechless, at Kent. Finally he whispered, "The Wizard?" and fingered his jersey. "Wow!"

Over Nick's head, Kent grinned at Mallory, then winked at her for the second time that evening. Oh, darn, that wink would be the death of her, she thought as she smiled back at him. She felt her cheeks heat, and as they followed the usher to the clubhouse, wondered if she could be falling in love with Kent all over again. And this time, with barely a touch between them.

Then suddenly they stood at the dressing room door. "Sacred ground," Kent murmured, and Nick's eyes got even wider as the usher knocked and stepped inside, affording them the briefest glimpse of several players, now in street clothes, standing nearby. A loud laugh sounded from inside the dressing room, and Mallory watched her son take everything in.

Suddenly the door opened and out stepped a big man

with broad shoulders and chest, and intense brown eyes.
And a goatee. On another man it might have looked
incongruous; on him it looked…macho.

Mallory could hardly believe this was really happening. Here was Nick's idol, Clay Parker, in the flesh.

He strode straight to the boy and put out his hand.
"Nick! Clay Parker. Hello there."

Nick gulped, but he put out his hand. "Hello, Mr.
Parker." Then with a show of manners that made Mallory's
heart swell with pride, he introduced her and Kent.

The legendary pitcher chatted with Nick for a good
ten minutes, asking about his Little League experience,
praising him for his courage in dealing with his illness
and wishing him a full recovery. Finally, he took a
baseball, a scuffed one, from his pocket, scribbled his
name on it and handed it to Nick.

The usher, who stood leaning against the wall,
stepped forward and said to Nick, "Want me to take a
picture of you and your family with Mr. Parker?"

"Good idea." Kent handed over his camera. "Take a
couple."

Afterward Parker left and Nick stood still, gazing
starry-eyed until the pitcher turned the corner and was
out of sight.

"Time to go, Nick," Mallory said, and he ambled
silently between them, turning the ball Parker had given
him over and over in his hand.

He was quiet on the way home and Mallory thought
he'd fallen asleep, but when she turned to look, she saw
him still holding his prized baseball, tracing Parker's
signature with his finger.

At home, his feet dragged as they walked to the door,

but he straightened and offered his hand to Kent. "Thank you, Dr. Berger."

Kent smiled. "It was a pleasure."

Kent had been so generous. He'd given Nick—given both of them—an unforgettable night. Mallory knew she needed to do more than just say thank you and walk inside.

She wasn't sure it was the *smart* thing to do, but she knew it was the *right* thing. She turned to Kent and said, "Why don't you come in and have a cup of coffee?"

Chapter Nine

"Thanks, I'd like coffee," Kent said and followed them inside. "Decaf if you have it."

"I do. I'll put it on," Mallory said. "Nick, want some milk?"

Nick yawned. "No, thank you."

"How about bed then? You look worn out."

"Okay. Thanks again, Dr. Berger." Yawning wider, he shuffled toward the bedroom.

"Not a word of complaint about bedtime. He must be exhausted," Mallory murmured, then headed for the kitchen. "Be right back."

In the kitchen she got the coffee out. Well, she'd done it: put herself alone with Kent, without Nick.

The coffee spoon slipped out of her nervous hands and coffee grounds scattered over the counter. She swept them into a paper towel, and it, too, fell out of her grasp. Now the floor was a mess. Heck with it. She kicked at the grounds with her foot, then picked up the spoon. She put it in the dishwasher and got out a clean one.

Why was she so nervous? When he accepted her invitation to come in for coffee, Kent's smile was easy and polite. No hungry looks had passed between them. To be truthful, if anyone was guilty of casting a few longing glances, she was.

Carefully she measured the coffee and started it brewing, then opened the refrigerator and got out a cherry pie she'd picked up this morning on a whim.

Whim? Or had she been planning this?

And what was "this" anyway?

Just a pleasant conversation, nothing more.

She left the coffee perking and went into Nick's bedroom to check on him. He was already asleep, his signed baseball clutched in his hand. One foot stuck out from under the sheet and she tucked it in gently. She touched her son's cheek, breathed in his little-boy scent and whispered, "'Night, sweetie." His only answer was a snore.

As she returned to the kitchen, soft rock music met her ears. Kent had turned on the radio. Destiny's Child was playing. She and Kent had always liked the same music. She remembered a night they'd danced under the stars to "That's the Way Love Goes" by Janet Jackson. A full moon, the summer breeze…

Forcing her mind back to the present, she slid slices of pie onto plates, poured coffee and arranged everything on a tray. She frowned at the chipped dessert plates and unmatched mugs that came with her furnished apartment. At home she had pretty china, a set of matching mugs.

These were fine. She and Jeremy Spellman's mother Tamara drank from them all the time. She didn't need anything fancy.

When she came into the living room, she found Kent thumbing through a magazine. From her meager selection, mostly copies of *Ranger Rick*, he'd picked up a copy of *Parents*. How ironic.

He looked up when she set the tray down on the coffee table. "Thanks. That pie looks good. Did you bake it?"

Mallory laughed. "I'm a florist and a gardener, not a cook."

Keen brown eyes studied her. "How did you get into the florist business? It's a far cry from what you said you wanted to do."

Got sidetracked along the way. "I love growing flowers. Sometimes I use flowers from my garden in arrangements for the temple. I met Lauri, my business partner, at services soon after she moved to Valerosa. We got to be friends and fellow garden club members, and we'd work out together, too. One morning on side-by-side exercise bikes, we had this mutual inspiration— 'Let's open a florist shop.'" She laughed. "That should be accompanied by the sound of trumpets." Kent's answering smile warmed her and she went on. "Six months later we gave birth to Buds and Blossoms."

She smiled fondly, and Kent asked, "How's your offspring coming along?"

"Well," Mallory said, "not to boast, of course, but Valerosa had a total of six flower shops, and we're closing in on number two."

"Working toward number one."

"Exactly." She was relaxed now. Kent had chosen a safe topic. Professional, not personal. Staying with it, she asked, "What about you? What brought you to cancer? I thought you always wanted to be a pediatrician?"

His lips curved. "I did. You used to say it was because I was a kid at heart."

"Did I?" Mallory asked lightly, pretending not to remember. But she did. She remembered...everything.

Kent picked up his mug, drank, set it down again. "I'd been in practice a year when I had a young patient, a girl of three named Kimberly, who contracted leukemia. I couldn't treat her, not in a regular pediatric practice, and that frustrated the hell out of me. And challenged me."

Mallory nodded. That was definitely the Kent she'd known. The quick mind, the drive to be the best. Not just in medicine but in *healing*.

"Kimberly's two older brothers were patients of mine, too, so I kept up with her progress. I started reading everything I could on pediatric cancer, talked Kim's doctor at the University of Chicago Hospital into letting me shadow him on weekends, and finally took the plunge and applied for a two-year fellowship at Sloan-Kettering."

"New York. That must have been exciting."

Kent set his coffee mug down. "The medicine was. I didn't see much of the city, didn't care much for the crowds and the noise."

Mallory noticed the way he gripped the mug, saw his lips thin and remembered that he and his wife had divorced soon after the move to Houston. He'd said his desire for a family was the main cause for the split but there must have been other issues, too. A model wouldn't have wanted to leave New York.

Don't go there. Easy, because she didn't want to know more about his marriage. She wanted to know other things. Silly things, personal things. *Do you like to sleep late on Sundays and cuddle in bed? Do you sing in the shower? Do you like popcorn with butter, or without?* She cleared her throat. "Working here at Gaines Memorial must be the challenge you wanted."

"It is. There's always more to learn, though. Next week I'm going to a conference in Philadelphia on future trends in pediatric cancer."

Going to Philadelphia. Mallory hoped he didn't notice her dismay. She felt as if she'd been pushed off the high wire and was flailing around in the air with no safety net beneath her.

He looked up just then from cutting off a bite of pie and read her completely. "Josh Ratcliff will be seeing my patients. We'll go over the charts before I leave."

Mallory tried to make her nod convincing.

She knew she didn't succeed when Kent continued. "He's very competent, has a great bedside manner with kids."

Mallory forced a smile. "Practically your double."

"Right, Mom. And Philadelphia's just a phone call away. Give me a notepad and I'll write down my hotel."

"Okay." She got her pad of Post-it notes for him. He scribbled something and handed it back. She frowned at the writing. "You're staying at a pink harem?"

"Hyatt. Park Hyatt."

"Sure looks like Pink Harem to me."

Kent chuckled. "Doctor's chicken-scratching. Anyway, you'll know where to find me. And so will Dr. Ratcliff."

Mallory put the note by the phone along with her list of things to do next week. Knowing where Kent would be was comforting, but she wouldn't call him. Unless there was an emergency.

She returned to her chair. "Are you speaking at the conference?"

He nodded. Of course, he was. She was proud of him for that. No, she wasn't. She had no reason to be proud. "Proud" was a proprietary word. She was *pleased,* happy she'd chosen an outstanding doctor for Nick.

Unable to think of anything neutral to talk about, Mallory concentrated on her cherry pie, savoring the combination of tart and sweet rolling over her tongue. She felt Kent's gaze on her and looked up. She swallowed. "What?" she asked.

"Just wondering what your life is like at home," he said.

This was veering toward the personal, but she shrugged. "Pretty average. I have a nice house with a garden. School nights I come home from the store, supervise homework. In the summer our world revolves around Little League. Friday nights we have dinner with my parents, go to services."

Kent looked thoughtful. "Different from what you used to dream about."

Mallory's lips thinned and she shook her head. "The doctorate in psychology, the thriving practice, travel. That's what I *thought* my dream was. Now I know that I got what I really wanted after all." She took the last bite of pie and pushed her plate away. "I've had the blessings of an ordinary life. I hope I get them back again."

Kent's eyes softened. "You will."

"If you say so, I believe you."

"Good." He glanced at his watch. "I should be going."

They rose and walked together to the door. "I can't thank you enough for tonight," Mallory said. "Nick will never forget this. Neither will I."

"It was my pleasure," he said. He leaned toward her and brushed a light kiss over her cheek.

The kiss was over in an instant, but her breath caught. So did his.

Their gazes locked for a long moment, fraught with uncertainty and tension.

Mallory watched his eyes heat, darken. She couldn't look away, couldn't move.

And then with a moan, or a curse, she couldn't tell which, he reached for her and pulled her into his arms.

Chapter Ten

This was what she wanted, what she'd longed for: Kent's arms wrapped around her and his lips covering hers. A small voice inside whispered, "No," but Mallory ignored it. She heard nothing but Kent's voice murmuring her name as he tightened his hold and pressed her against his chest where his heart beat strong and steady.

How long had it been? Centuries, millenniums, since she'd felt the roughness of his cheeks against hers, the strong bones of his jaw. And his mouth, that skillful mouth that could tease and tantalize, coax and seduce.

She curled her arms around his neck, ran her fingers through his hair, remembering the texture, the waviness. She traced the outline of his ear, heard his breath catch at her touch. She broke the kiss and buried her head in the hollow of his neck, feeling flesh and bone, tasting the old familiar flavor, licking the saltiness of his skin.

He kissed her hair, lifted it and kissed her nape, sending shivers along her spine. Then he urged her head up so he could take her mouth again. His tongue teased her lips apart, then dove inside to capture hers. She met him, and long lost memories surfaced as their tongues touched, shifted, rubbed and rolled, as their bodies had years ago. He took the kiss deeper, his tongue plunging—

From the street outside a car horn honked and the sounds of traffic intruded into their private world. They broke apart.

How long had they stood like this, locked in each other's embrace? Time had stopped. And now it started again.

"Kent," she murmured, not sure what else to say.

He touched her cheek. "I want you."

She took a step back, automatically glanced over her shoulder toward the room where Nick slept. "I—"

He laid his finger over her lips. "Shh, not now. But we'll find a time. Soon."

He took her hands and lifted them to his lips, kissed the palms softly. "Good night."

"Good night," she echoed as he opened the door and shut it behind him. She put a hand to her swollen lips and listened to his footsteps die away.

In a daze, she undressed, checked on Nick again, then climbed into her bed. She lay on her back, staring at the ceiling. Again she touched her lips, tracing them with a finger.

Now there was much more than a touch between her and Kent. A kiss, as incendiary as it was unexpected.

Or was it?

Hadn't this been building since the first time they'd talked in the doctors' lounge in the middle of the night? Hadn't she wanted this, yearned for his touch from the first moment she'd seen him in her son's hospital room?

She had, and wasn't she a fool for wanting? There was too much between them—too many years, too many unanswered questions. She'd forgotten too easily what had happened before. Shouldn't she have learned from that?

She turned on her side, pulled the sheets around her shoulders and squeezed her eyes shut. The hum of the air conditioner usually put her to sleep, but tonight it only annoyed her. She turned over to face the hall and saw she'd forgotten to turn off the light in the kitchen. Unwilling to get up, she turned to the other side.

She was tired but sleep wouldn't come. Memories flooded her mind. The last time she'd kissed Kent, right before he left to meet his mentor at the medical conference in Milan. How she'd clung to him, hating to let him go even though he'd be back in a couple of weeks.

While he was gone, she'd joined her family and Dean's on a trip through the South. Every night she'd counted the days until Kent's return. Every day she pretended to be having a good time.

She remembered Nashville, going with Dean to Opryland Amusement Park. The Ferris wheel. And her first inkling that she was pregnant. That horrible queasy feeling, and the dizziness, as if she were Dorothy in *The Wizard of Oz*, spinning through the tornado. Dean had been concerned, but Mallory had laughed off that first round of nausea, attributing it to too many Goo Goo

Supremes, clusters of marshmallows and peanuts, as rich and gooey as their name.

But the next morning when the smell of coffee brought another attack, and she realized her period was a week late, she knew.

And felt a sudden fear. Had that ride on the Ferris wheel hurt the baby? She needed to see a doctor. When they got home, she'd find an excuse to drive to Dallas, where no one knew her. She couldn't possibly walk into Dr. Sanders's office and ask for a pregnancy test.

But why wait to go to Dallas? Why not Nashville?

She confided in Dean, they picked an obstetrician at random from the Yellow Pages, and when the doctor— she couldn't remember his name now, only his voice with its Southern drawl—had congratulated them on the pregnancy, she hadn't been surprised. But she'd felt a tiny twinge of anxiety, and Dean had added to it when he'd asked, "What will you do?"

She had Kent's number in Milan, but she didn't want to tell him the news on the phone. "We'll be home Monday and Kent will be back on Wednesday. He'll call as soon as he lands in New York, then fly to Dallas. I'll tell him when I pick him up at the airport there and we'll just get married a little earlier than we planned."

On Wednesday she waited by the phone. But it didn't ring.

His plane was delayed, she told herself, but when she called the airline, she learned his flight had landed on time. She waited all day for a call, the pinch of anxiety expanding until it took over her whole body.

The next day, as soon as her mother left to visit a congregant in the hospital, she dug out the number Kent had given her and called his Milan hotel, her hands sweating so badly she could barely hold the phone.

There was no Kent Berger registered.

"There must be a mistake." Mallory forced herself to speak slowly so the clerk could understand. "He gave me this number. C-could you check the records?"

"A minute, *signorina*."

The minute stretched to two, then three before the clerk returned. "My apologies, *signorina*," he said in heavily accented English. "Dr. Berger was indeed a guest here, but he checked out three days ago."

"Three days?" Mallory sank into a chair. Her voice shook as she asked, "Did he say where he was going?"

"Ah, *scuso, signorina*. I do not know. I was on holiday when the doctor was a guest."

Mallory bit her lip. What could have happened? "Is Dr. Wilson still at the hotel?" Maybe he could tell her.

"I will check."

Again she waited. Longer this time. She wiped her hands on her shorts, counted the seconds as voices in Italian sounded through the staticky background.

She heard the sound of the receiver being lifted and the clerk said, "Signorina Wilson is no longer in residence."

She'd waited all this time for the information about the wrong person. Annoyed, Mallory said, "Dr. Wilson. Charles Wilson."

"Please, I could find no record of a Dr. Wilson." A hint of embarrassment came across the wire. "The room was occupied by a Signorina Clare Wilson. She and Dr. Berger checked out togeth— Ah, at the same time."

Mallory felt a bolt of electricity shoot into her heart. She let the phone slip from her numb fingers.

Kent had been in Milan, all right. And maybe there was a medical conference. But the rest was lies. Everything he'd told her, from "I love you" to "I'll see you again" was a lie. The truth was that he was traveling Europe with a woman, not the middle-aged physician he'd described. And worst was that Mallory had actually been gullible enough to believe him.

Even now, eleven years later, lying on her bed, she felt the sting of betrayal.

And here she was, falling into the same quagmire all over again. A proverb of her father's came into her mind: The best armor is to keep out of range.

Well, she'd violated that one, big-time. She'd not only been "in range," she'd practically been in bed again with the man who'd once betrayed her.

She kicked at the sheet, turned her pillow over and punched it. From now on, she'd remember her father's adage and keep out of Kent's way. She could trust him unwaveringly with her son's life, but she didn't dare trust him with her heart.

The following Monday, a hot, cloudless day, Mallory and Tamara decided to take Nick and Jeremy on a sightseeing trip to Galveston. They took Tamara's car and left after lunch, planning to be back by dinnertime so they wouldn't have to deal with a crowded restaurant.

The boys were in high spirits, giggling in the backseat, arguing over baseball teams, lowering their voices to tell jokes. Judging from their snickers, Mallory figured those were ten-year-old versions of dirty jokes.

She and Tamara talked about home. The Spellmans lived in San Antonio, where Jeremy's two older siblings were staying with grandparents. Her husband Daniel drove in every other weekend. "I hope we can go home for a visit soon," Tamara said longingly, then chuckled. "With Dan's housekeeping skills, I bet our house is a sewer, even without the boys there." She sighed. "You'd think, with all of today's gadgets and products, even a man could make the floors shine and the dishes sparkle."

"Have you seen that dumb new reality show, *Mommy Survivor?*" Mallory asked. "I caught it the other day."

"The show that puts moms and their kids in a low-tech environment for a month? No TV, no computers, no cell phones. I think they should call it *Mommy Goes Insane*," Tamara said.

"Or *Back to the 1940s*," Mallory suggested. "There was a time when families didn't have all those gizmos. Might be a myth, but I've heard our ancestors managed anyway."

"What do those TV producers really know about survival?" Tamara said with a bitter laugh.

"Not much. Not the way we do."

"Yeah," Tamara agreed. "What we're doing every day—*this* is a real fight for survival."

"With real lives on the line."

"At least we have each other." Faced with the immensity of their battles, they both fell silent.

Tamara turned onto the Gulf Freeway leading to Galveston, which was fifty miles to the south. Already billboards for boats and beach houses were appearing along the freeway feeder.

After a few minutes Tamara said, "The boys are doing well right now, thank God." When Mallory nodded, her friend added, "I bet Nick would have willed himself into remission to get to that baseball game."

"For sure."

Tamara glanced at Mallory. "Nice of Dr. Berger to get the tickets. Is he a relative?"

Immediately Mallory's guard went up. She shifted in her seat. "No."

"Oh, I just thought I saw a family resemblance between him and Nick."

Thank heavens she wasn't driving, Mallory thought, or she might have plowed into a truck.

Blithely, Tamara continued. "Can't be hair, of course," she said with a chuckle. "It's something about their eyes…."

Hands clenched in her lap, Mallory managed a wooden smile. "They both have brown ones." She'd hoped only she could see the resemblance because she was looking for it. Obviously it was apparent to others, too. She shrugged. "We're not related. I met Dr. Berger a few years ago when he was in Valerosa." No need to say exactly how many years.

"Slap me if I'm out of line, but do you two have a…history?"

"History?" Only force of will kept Mallory from answering in a squeak. For one brief moment, she was tempted to blurt out everything, but she swallowed the words. She'd never confided in anyone but Dean. Now wasn't the time to start. "No, just an acquaintance."

"Is that why you took Nick to him?"

"No, our doctor recommended him, and I remembered hearing he was good. I'm glad we came."

"Me, too."

A guffaw sounded from behind them, and Tamara flipped on the radio. "Let's have some music and drown out those little lunatics in the backseat."

The rest of the drive passed without incident, and soon they were approaching the high bridge separating Galveston Island from the mainland. The boys stopped their chatter and took in the sights as they drove across the bridge.

"Water!" Nick exclaimed, peering at the blue-gray waters of the gulf. "It's all around us."

"Duh, we're on an island," Jeremy said.

"Oh, yeah." Nick craned his neck. "Look at all the birds. Can we feed 'em, Mom?"

"Sure." They made a quick stop at a convenience store for bread, drove to the sea wall and got out. The smell of sand and salt met them, and a soft gulf breeze cooled the afternoon heat. The boys threw bread crumbs to an increasing throng of squawking seagulls.

"Can we wade in the water?" Jeremy asked.

"Not allowed, remember," his mother answered.

Mallory sighed as she watched the surf. Maybe someday when Nick was well, they'd come back.

They took the ferry to Bolivar Island and let the boys sit on the fenders and watch the boats, then they headed back to Houston.

Back in their apartment, Mallory made Nick a sandwich and let him eat in front of the TV while she went back into the kitchen for her daily call to her parents.

When she finished talking, she found Nick sleeping. The remote had slipped from his hand and his head lolled to the side. "Bedtime, Nicky," she said and put her hand on his shoulder.

He was hot. Too hot.

Alarmed, Mallory hurried into the bedroom for the thermometer. "Wake up, Nick," she said sternly and his eyes opened momentarily, then shut again.

She shook him gently. "Open your mouth, baby. I need to take your temperature."

"Mmh," he said but obediently opened for her.

It read 103.7. That couldn't be right. "Open again, Nick."

"Don' wanna."

"Nicholas." She shoved the thermometer in, waited for the beep. This time it read 104.

"Oh, my God." She ran to the phone and called Dr. Ratcliff's answering service.

In less than two minutes he called back. "I'll meet you at the emergency room," he said.

"Okay." She urged Nick out of his chair and with her arm around him, got him to the car. His skin was burning hot. He lay in the backseat, his breath wheezing in and out while she drove and prayed.

She pulled into a parking spot near the emergency room, snagged a wheelchair that someone had left by the curb and managed to prod Nick out of the car and into it. Not so many years ago, she thought with a pang, she could have picked him up and carried him in. Now he was too heavy. Before long he'd be a teenager. Oh, God, would he make it, have a Bar Mitzvah, a first date, a senior prom? *Don't think about that now. Just get him inside, and hope we don't have to wait.*

They didn't. Dr. Ratcliff arrived minutes after they did. With calm efficiency, he examined the lethargic youngster, then turned to Mallory. "His fever's pretty high, so we'll admit him and start antibiotics." He moved aside as a white-coated gentleman from the lab arrived with needles and syringes, and proceeded to draw blood.

"What's wrong with him?" Mallory asked, clenching her hands.

"Probably just an infection." Before she could ask, he added, "Happens all the time. Nothing to get too upset over, but we like to watch these things."

Within a short time Nick was settled in a room. Mallory decided not to call her parents until she had more information. No point in frightening them, too.

As night came on, she curled in a chair in the corner of the room and watched the drip, drip, drip of the IV as it fed antibiotics into Nick's vein. She wanted answers, not the vague, "It happens all the time," but maybe that's all Dr. Ratcliff could give her.

What had she done wrong? she berated herself. Had Nick gotten overheated? Had they been too close to the birds? Had she forgotten to give him some of his meds?

The nurse came in around ten, took Nick's vital signs and said his temperature was dropping. That was a good sign, Mallory knew, but she also knew his fever could spike up again in a heartbeat.

Again she reviewed everything that had happened in the last day, then the days before. Could he have picked up some kind of bug at the baseball game? He'd worn his mask in the ballpark, only taken it off for a minute, for the picture with Clay Parker.

She was scared and lonely, and she wanted someone to lean on. She felt tears coming and blinked them back. No matter how she felt, she had to be strong. If Nick woke and saw her crying, he'd surely be frightened.

Of all the times for Kent to be out of town, why did it have to be now?

Chapter Eleven

Kent sat in the Library Lounge on the nineteenth floor of the Park Hyatt with his old friends, Rod and Carol Shaver. He swirled his brandy as he glanced at the quiet elegance of the room and the lights of Philadelphia shimmering below. "We've come a long way since med school, buddy."

Rod laughed. "Yeah, food barely fit for human consumption, no sleep, studying till we were half-blind. Those were the days."

"Remember the dump we lived in? The walls were so thin—"

"—we could hear every creak of the bedsprings next door whenever George Franklin entertained."

"Yeah," Kent agreed, "and he entertained six nights

out of seven. Must've gone through three sets of bed-springs that year."

"What I remember," Carol said primly, "is the stacks of dirty dishes in your kitchen. You never washed."

"Sure we did," Rod said. "Whenever we ran out." He pointed a thumb at his wife. "*She* makes me wash after every meal," he said and sighed dramatically. "I've been domesticated."

"And you love it," Kent observed.

"Right." Rod reached for Carol's hand, lifted it to his lips. "We're expecting."

"Again?"

"Number three," Carol said.

"God, that's great."

"You'll have to come and visit us in Boston and meet the horde," Rod said.

"I'd like that."

"Might seem dull for a bachelor like you," Rod observed.

His friends apparently thought he was a man-about-town, but in reality his life seemed pale and lonely in comparison to theirs. He raised his snifter and took a swallow of brandy. "The single life leaves something to be desired."

They talked for a while longer, shaking their heads over the coincidence that although Rod had planned on being a neurologist and Kent had started as a pediatrician, they'd both ended up in oncology, and both specialized in children.

"Another brandy, sir?" the waiter asked.

Kent looked down in surprise to see that his glass was empty. He started to order another, but changed his mind. "I'd better call it a night," he told his friends, paid his tab and took the elevator down to the eighth floor.

As it descended, he felt a vague uneasiness, a feeling that something wasn't quite right. In his room he glanced at the phone. No messages. Nevertheless he picked up the receiver and placed a call to Josh Ratcliff.

He heard the sounds of talk and laughter in the background when Josh picked up. "It's Kent. Sorry if I've disturbed an evening out."

"No problem," his colleague said. "What can I do for you?"

"Just had a feeling I should check in. One of those intuitive things."

"Let's see. Amy Ellinger's starting a rash, and Nick Brenner spiked a fever. I put him in for observation."

Kent felt a sudden, surprising stab of anxiety. "What time was he admitted?"

"Around seven. Fever's already coming down."

"Good. Thanks." He hung up and sat staring at the receiver in his hand. He'd told Mallory to call him, just to talk, but she hadn't. The first two days in Philadelphia, he'd hoped she would but he wasn't really surprised that he didn't hear from her. But now, with Nick sick...

He called the hotel operator and double-checked his mailbox. Nothing. He dialed the hospital, got Nick's room phone number and put in a call. As the phone began to ring, a thought jumped into his mind. Mallory had already gotten medical information from Josh; maybe she'd called someone else for comfort and reassurance. Maybe there was someone in Valerosa or someplace nearby whose voice she wanted to hear instead of his. She'd kissed him back readily enough the other night, but she'd done that years ago and there'd been another man then, too.

He almost disconnected, but as his finger reached the button, Mallory picked up. "Hello?" Her voice sounded shaky.

"Hi," he said.

"Kent!" She sounded relieved. "I'm so glad you called. I needed to talk to you."

Kent tucked the phone under his cheek and loosened his tie. "You have my number."

"I know, but—"

"It's okay." He noted perversely that she said she needed to *talk to* him rather than saying she needed him. Big difference, but with Nick ill, he forced himself to overlook it. "How's Nick?" he asked.

"Sleeping. His fever's down a little." She paused, then asked, "How did you kn— Oh, I guess you spoke to Dr. Ratcliff."

"A few minutes ago."

"Oh, Kent." She sounded close to tears. "What did I do wrong?"

He'd heard other mothers say the same words, but hearing Mallory's plaintive question made his heart hurt. "Mallory—"

"We went to Galveston today. It was hot, or maybe the ball game—"

"Mallory," he said firmly. "You didn't do anything. Kids with leukemia get sudden fevers all the time."

"But why?" Her voice rose in frustration.

"Sometimes from chemo, sometimes from bacteria in their own bodies."

She sighed. "That's what Dr. Ratcliff said."

Kent smiled as he plumped a pillow against the head-board and leaned back. "He's right."

"Hearing it from you makes me believe it."

"The important thing is that the fever's coming down," he reminded her.

"I know that. I...I'm sorry for whining at you and asking the same questions you have to know I already asked Dr. Ratcliff."

"It's okay. I'd be just as worried if it were my kid." When she made no comment, he said, "What else can I tell you?"

"Um, maybe you could distract me. Tell me about Philadelphia."

"Haven't seen much of the city this trip. The conference is great though."

"How was your talk?" she asked. "Well received, I'm sure."

"It's nice to have a fan club. Actually the speech did go pretty well."

"Anything else?" Her voice was calmer now.

"An NFL player is speaking at the banquet tomorrow. His child had leukemia."

"Had?" Her voice tensed again.

"Had and got well." He heard her relieved sigh. "Maybe I can get his autograph for Nick."

"He'd love that. He's been sleeping with the baseball. He even brought it with him to the hospital."

"Bill Buckner autographed my program at a Cubs game when I was a kid," Kent said. "I slept with it under my pillow for months." He kicked off his shoes. "I think it's still around somewhere."

"Boys and baseball. I guess some things never change."

"Tell me what you've been doing," he said.

"Oh, gardening, reading, playing poker. You know, it's really an interesting game. I've started watching poker tournaments on television."

She giggled, and he smiled, knowing she was herself again. He shut his eyes and pictured her watching her son. She'd be curled up in a chair in the half light, eyes fixed on Nick, her shoes kicked off. Then he imagined her as she'd been the other night, warm and soft in his arms. "I want to see you when I get back."

"I... Oh, here's the nurse." A voice sounded and Mallory said, "Can you wait? She's taking his vital signs."

"Sure."

After a few minutes Mallory came back on the line. "Fever's down to ninety-nine and a half."

"Good. He's going to be fine."

"Thanks, doctor," she said around a yawn.

"Sounds like you're tired," Kent said. "Have I distracted you enough that you can sleep?"

Another yawn. "I think so."

"Good night, then," he said. "Take care." He hung up, then realized she hadn't said if she'd see him again.

She would. On that, he was determined.

Nick bounced back from his episode of fever. Faster than she did, Mallory thought ruefully. Although he was still on antibiotics, he seemed none the worse for wear, while she was worn out from the stress and worry.

And then Kent called. "How do you feel about dinosaurs?"

"Umm, I dunno. I've never met one."

"Want to?"

Mallory laughed. "Okay, doc, what are we talking about?"

"There's a new exhibit coming to the Houston Museum of Natural Science: robotic dinosaurs, bones, information on paleontology. I know Nick's probably past the 'dinos are my life' stage, but this is supposed to be awesome. Want to go?"

She glanced back at Nick, who was absorbed in the latest Harry Potter book. "Won't it be crowded?"

"There's a private showing for museum members tomorrow night."

"And of course you're a member."

"Since today."

"You just joined?" she asked. "Because of this show? How can I turn you down?"

"Exactly what I thought. I'll pick you up at seven."

Mallory hung up, knowing she was getting in deeper than she'd intended. But she was lonely and Kent was so charming. And so kind to do this for them.

She'd hold tight to her heart. She'd have to.

She reminded herself of that the next evening when she looked out her front window and saw Kent drive up. How many other people here happened to be looking out their windows, too, she asked herself. Soon the apartment's gossip mill would be going like wildfire. Why hadn't she lied and told Tamara she and Kent were cousins? That would make evenings like this so much easier to explain. Why hadn't she *thought?* But then when had she ever been her usual sensible self when it came to Kent?

Nick, his mask now decorated with dinosaur stickers, scurried to open the door. They all exchanged greetings and then they were on their way.

They parked in the museum garage, where all the floors had dinosaur names, then made their way inside the nearly empty building and found the exhibit. Gigantic creatures moved, roared and bared their teeth while visitors strolled around ogling them. Nick's mouth dropped open as he inched closer to the T rex. "Man, these are so real."

"Scarily real," Mallory agreed, then murmured to Kent, "I'm going to have nightmares."

He moved closer. "I could hold your hand."

She looked down at his fingers inches from hers, felt his breath against her cheek. Her heart sped up. "Kent, don't," she whispered.

"Why not?"

"Because—" She couldn't think of a single reason. And he knew it.

He chuckled softly and stepped away but his eyes stayed on her, their gaze intense. He was seducing her, here beside the prehistoric beasts. This was the most unromantic place she could think of. And yet her pulse was pounding, her skin flushed.

Nick sauntered back to them. "Did you see the pterodactyl's teeth?"

"Yes, terrifying. Don't wander off, Nick. Stay with us."

Kent's eyes sparkled with amusement. "Coward," he mouthed.

"Rat."

"What rat?" Nick asked.

"Nothing," Mallory said. "I was talking to myself. Let's take a look at the bones."

For the rest of the hour they wandered about, enjoying the exhibit. When they arrived back home, Mallory kept

Nick firmly by her side. Luckily, Kent said he had early rounds and after a quick good night, he left.

The next morning Nick went in for a blood test. As soon as Mallory sat down in the waiting room, she felt curious eyes on her. Within a few minutes Karen LeMay scooted over to sit beside her. "Who was that hunk who picked you up last night? I could swear he looked like Dr. Berger."

Of course Karen just "happened" to be looking out the window when Kent's car drove up. Mallory sighed inwardly and counted to ten. "It *was* Dr. Berger." Before Karen could ask, she added, "Our families are friends." Okay, she hadn't said that to Tamara, but she did mention she'd met him in Valerosa so it made sense.

"Is his father a minister, too?"

Mallory gave Karen a blank look. "I beg your pardon?"

"Isn't your father a minister…a Jewish one?"

"A rabbi."

"So does Dr. B.'s father do that, too?"

"No," Mallory said. She actually had no idea what Kent's father did so she made up a job. "He's a CPA." Mallory grabbed a magazine and hoped Karen would read the signal that she didn't want to talk anymore. Apparently she did, leaving Mallory pretending to read *Popular Mechanics.* Great.

After a bit Catherine Garland stuck her head out the door. "Mrs. Brenner, may I speak with you?"

A familiar knot of fear tightening in her chest, Mallory tossed the magazine aside and jumped up to follow Catherine inside and down a hall to a small room that held a table and a couple of chairs. "Is something wrong?"

Catherine set a folder on the table. "We've heard back on you and your family's blood screenings."

Although the nurse's face was impassive, Mallory was sure the news wasn't good. "And?" she asked.

"No matches." Catherine gave her a minute to absorb the news, then said, "But remember, we've only just begun. First of all, can you think of any relatives who haven't been tested?"

"No."

"Well, lots of kids end up with unrelated donors." At Mallory's look of alarm, she added, "And they do just fine." She glanced at the folder on the table.

"So what do we do now?" Mallory asked. It was always best to focus on what was possible, after all.

"Well, since you're looking for a donor of Eastern European extraction, you may want to make an appeal to the Jewish community in Valerosa and in Houston as well. And at the same time, you can start a registry search."

"I'll do that," Mallory said. "I don't suppose you know how long that will take."

Catherine shook her head. "I can inform the registry for you right away."

"Thanks."

As Mallory left the office, she repeated Catherine's words to herself: they'd only just begun. But her muscles were tight with tension. She'd just gotten over the fever scare, and now this. She felt like a cartoon character whose head pokes out of a hole in the ground and each time it does, a huge hammer bops it and knocks it back.

When Nick was ready, they went straight home and she called her father and got the name of the editor of Houston's weekly *Jewish-American Journal.* She called him, gave the needed information and he assured her an appeal would go out in the next issue. Mallory thanked him and hung up the phone.

She stared out the apartment window at the summer sky and wondered what unknown person would give her child a chance at life.

She sighed heavily. She'd lied to Catherine this morning. There *was* another relative, but she hoped to God she'd never have to use him.

Kent.

Chapter Twelve

Tamara Spellman took a sip of iced tea, then set her glass on Mallory's kitchen table. "I'm going stir-crazy," she said. "I need to get away from here. And I miss the rest of my family. Since Jeremy's in remission, I think I'll take him home for the weekend."

Mallory glanced at the clean but drab walls of her apartment. How she'd love to spend a night in her own bed, smell the perfume of her own garden and eat one of her mother's Sabbath meals. "Sounds great. I'd do the same thing, but Valerosa's too far."

"Come with us."

"Thanks, but you see me every day. You need some time with Daniel and your other kids."

"Send Nick, then."

Mallory shook her head. "Oh, I couldn't."

"What's wrong? Separation problems?"

Mallory drew a circle on the table with the moisture from the glass she held. "Sort of. Nick had that bout of fever, and it scared me."

"The fever's over," Tamara said. "You can't live your life being scared. Nick can't, either, and if *you're* afraid, it rubs off."

"You're right, Ms. Psychologist," Mallory said. "You sound like my dad."

"So let Nick come. The other day I heard Jeremy tell Nick he wished he could go home and he wanted Nick to come and visit. Besides, you could use a break from caregiving."

Mallory hesitated, frowned down at the table and tried to make up her mind.

"Call Dr. Berger and ask him what he thinks," Tamara suggested.

Mallory glanced at her watch. Kent had mentioned during Nick's checkup yesterday that he was going to Atlanta for a consult, leaving tomorrow and coming back late Saturday. In fact, he was probably gone already. But she could ask Catherine Garland. "Okay." She picked up the phone and dialed.

She was put through to Catherine. "Dr. Berger's heading out the door. I'll see if I can catch him."

"That's all right, I—" But Catherine had already put down the phone.

Mallory sighed. She felt uncomfortable talking to Kent in front of Tamara, in front of anyone. When his voice deepened and roughened as if they were alone in some secluded spot, she knew her face flushed and her eyes softened. Wouldn't Tamara notice? Casually, she turned so that her back was to her friend.

In a moment, Kent answered crisply. "Dr. Berger."

"Um, this is Mallory Brenner," she began.

Immediately his voice warmed. "Hi, Mallory Brenner."

Yes, she could feel her skin heat. She bit her lip. "I'm sorry Catherine troubled you but I, uh, have a question."

"And an audience, too, I bet."

"Right. Anyway, the Spellmans are going home for the weekend and they've invited Nick to come along. What do you think?"

"Sounds like a great idea to me. Both boys are in remission. As long as they keep the usual restrictions on crowds, diet, et cetera, why not?"

"I thought it might be too much…."

"You know my philosophy. Kids need to lead as normal a life as possible."

Mallory twisted a strand of hair around her finger. "I, um, guess I'll let him go then. Thanks for your time."

He chuckled softly. "All the time you want," he murmured, then hung up.

She waited a moment before she turned back to Tamara, just to be certain her cheeks were cool again. "He said yes," she said, returning to the table.

"Great. Let's tell the kids the good news."

As she went into Nick's room to get them, Mallory thought it was fortunate Kent was going to be out of town. Otherwise he might have construed her call as an invitation.

In spite of Kent's reassurance, Mallory was nervous about letting Nick go. Even a phone call to her parents didn't completely allay her fears, but Nick already knew about the trip. He and Jeremy had been talking all week about seeing Jeremy's pet corgi, driving past the Alamo and the dozens of other things they'd cram into the weekend. If she told him no at this point, he'd be devastated. He was counting the hours until Friday afternoon when Jeremy returned from his clinic appointment and they could be on their way.

Mallory tried to concentrate on plans for her own "weekend off." She'd indulge herself with a shopping trip—at least a window-shopping trip—to the Galleria, take in the newest exhibit at the Museum of Fine Arts, maybe see a movie. Lord, she hadn't been to a movie in months; theaters were rife with germs. She'd pick out a chick flick, something light and fluffy. She looked through the newspaper and found a new Julia Roberts movie that sounded perfect. By Thursday night she'd actually convinced herself she was looking forward to the weekend.

When Friday afternoon came, Nick dragged his duffel bag to the door, hurried back to his room to see if he'd forgotten anything, then sat by the window, tapping his foot impatiently. At four o'clock the Spellmans finally arrived.

"You have my phone number here and my cell phone, right?" Mallory asked nervously after Nick had given her an offhand hug and climbed into the backseat.

"On my PDA, in my purse, in the glove compartment, tattooed on my wrist," Tamara said. "He'll be fine. Say goodbye now."

Mallory laughed. "'Bye."

She watched them drive away and went inside. Forty-eight hours all to herself.

An Important Message from the Publisher

Dear Reader,

If you'd enjoy reading contemporary African-American love stories filled with drama and passion, then let us send you two free Kimani Romance™ novels. These books will keep it real with true-to-life African-American characters that turn up the heat and sizzle with passion.

By the way, you'll also get two surprise gifts with your two free books! Please enjoy the free books and gifts with our compliments...

Linda Gill

Publisher, Kimani Press

Peel off Seal and Place Inside...

PUBLISHERS FREE GIFT SEAL THANK YOU

We'd like to send you two free books to introduce you to our brand-new line – Kimani Romance™! These novels feature strong, sexy women, and African-American heroes that are charming, loving and true. Our authors fill each page with exceptional dialogue, exciting plot twists, and enough sizzling romance to keep you riveted until the very end!

KIMANI ROMANCE ... LOVE'S ULTIMATE DESTINATION

Two NEW Kimani Romance™ Novels
Two exciting surprise gifts

I have placed my
Editor's "thank you" Free Gifts
seal in the space provided at
right. Please send me 2 FREE
books, and my 2 FREE Mystery
Gifts. I understand that I am
under no obligation to purchase
anything further, as explained on
the back of this card.

PLACE
FREE GIFTS
SEAL
HERE

DETACH AND MAIL CARD TODAY!

168 XDL EF2K   **368 XDL EF2V**

FIRST NAME   LAST NAME

ADDRESS

APT #   CITY

STATE/PROV.   ZIP/POSTAL CODE

Thank You!

If offer card is missing write to: The Reader Service, 3010 Walden Ave., P.O. Box 1867, Buffalo, NY 14240-1867

POSTAGE WILL BE PAID BY ADDRESSEE

BUSINESS REPLY MAIL

FIRST-CLASS MAIL   PERMIT NO. 717-003   BUFFALO, NY

THE READER SERVICE
3010 WALDEN AVE
PO BOX 1867
BUFFALO NY 14240-9952

NO POSTAGE
NECESSARY
IF MAILED
IN THE
UNITED STATES

Two hours later she wondered how she'd get through the next forty-six. Bored and anxious, she turned on the six o'clock news. A traffic accident, a robbery at a convenience store, the prediction of a strong chance of rain—

The doorbell rang.

Mallory shot out of the chair and across the room. Something had happened. They were bringing Nick back! Sweat already pouring down her back, she yanked the door open.

Kent stood in the doorway.

Not Nick. She sagged against the wall, her legs threatening to fold under her. Black specks floated before her eyes.

Kent reached for her. "Mallory, what's wrong?"

She waved him away. "Nothing." She blinked hard and the tiny dots faded. She straightened but kept her hand on the door for support. "I thought something had happened to Nick."

"Sorry I scared you. I should have called first."

Mallory laughed weakly. "That would've scared me just as much." She blinked again. "You...you're not supposed to be here. I thought you were in Atlanta."

"I decided to come back early."

Still a little dazed, she frowned. "But what are you doing *here?*"

"Thought you might like a little support, Mom, with Nick gone for the first time." He smiled at her. "Looks like I was right. May I come in?"

"Oh, sorry. Sure." She stepped aside as he crossed the threshold. She didn't want his body to brush hers.

Liar! She wanted it too much.

But even though they didn't touch, she caught a whiff

of his cologne, an up-close view of his lashes and the dark stubble on his cheeks. He wore a tan polo shirt that made his skin look even more bronzed than usual, his shoulders even broader. Inside, he seemed to fill the room, his presence dominating.

"Why did you come back from Atlanta?" she asked.

"I finished sooner than I expected," he said, but his eyes caught hers and sent a silent message: *To be with you.*

And here they were. Alone, without Nick.

Quickly, Mallory asked, "Have you eaten?"

His lips quirked. "Are you inviting me to dinner?"

"With my cooking? Not a chance. But why don't we go out?" she suggested. "My treat." He'd been so nice to Nick, she owed him a meal. Besides, that would get them out of these close quarters that seemed to become closer by the second.

He grinned. "Thanks, I accept."

She needed to think of a restaurant that wasn't too showy or too fancy. "There's a place I've heard of near here called the Lark's Nest. Have you been there?"

"A couple of times. The food's good."

Mallory grabbed her purse and followed Kent outside to a dark blue Honda. "Where's your Jaguar?" she asked.

"I don't like to park it at the airport."

"So you're a two-car guy." She opened her door. "This one's a little staid."

"Exactly why I take it to the airport," he said, starting the engine.

As he drove, Mallory leaned back and studied Kent's profile. He was handsome, successful, charming. She wondered why he hadn't remarried. Maybe because he didn't like being tied to one woman. That had been his modus operandi years ago. Why should it have changed?

But she didn't want to dwell on the past or speculate about the future. She just wanted to concentrate on now. With Kent beside her, the fears about Nick lessened. She was free for the weekend and she intended to enjoy herself.

Having a good time with Kent wasn't hard, never had been. They sat at a quiet corner table on the restaurant's patio, surrounded by plants in terra cotta pots and the soft sound of piano music from inside.

Mallory indulged herself in a green salad with goat cheese and a glass of white wine. By unspoken agreement they stayed away from serious subjects—no medical discussions, nothing that even came close. They talked about the exhibit Mallory wanted to see at the art museum, about a movie that was being hyped as the blockbuster of the summer, about Kent's trip last year to Switzerland. The wine erased the last vestiges of worry from Mallory's mind. This was a reprise of "Life before Leukemia," except that Valerosa was hardly a haven for singles, so Mallory rarely dated, and now she sat across the table from a man who made her pulse pound with only a glance.

Mallory begged off dessert but Kent ordered strawberry shortcake. When it came, he tasted it and murmured, "You don't know what you're missing. Want a bite?"

"Sure." They both leaned forward and Kent brought the sweet-filled fork to her parted lips. She took a bite, then another. She shut her eyes to savor, not just the food but the giving of it. Being fed was…intimate.

"More?" Kent's voice was hoarse.

She opened her eyes, met his. "No, thank you."

They were silent as Kent finished his dessert, then signaled the waiter for the check, which Kent handed to Mallory with a flourish.

When they left the restaurant, Mallory asked, "Want to see a movie? The new Julia Roberts got three stars."

Kent rolled his eyes. "That movie's for women."

"A good reason for you to see it, Dr. Macho. You could learn something."

"Hah," he said. "What?"

"How to understand a woman's psyche, how to know what women want." She grinned at him. "Pay attention. There'll be a test afterward."

"One no man could pass," he said as they got into the car.

The nearby theater was crowded with weekend moviegoers. Mallory bought their tickets and they hurried in to find seats as the previews were ending.

In the dark with Kent beside her, Mallory could almost imagine they were back in Valerosa when they were both young and optimistic, ready to take on the world, side by side. They'd sat like this so many times back then.

Midway through the movie Kent stretched his arm across the back of her seat. He didn't pull her close but she wished he would. She wanted to rub against him like a contented cat. *Wow,* she chuckled to herself, *that must be the wine.*

When they left the theater, the sky was overcast. Dark clouds curtained the moon and stars. The air smelled of rain. Kent put his arm around Mallory's shoulder as they hurried to the car.

When they parked in front of her building and got out, he took her hand in his as they walked slowly toward the door and stood beneath the overhang. "Thanks for the dinner and the movie," Kent said.

"Thanks for keeping my mind off Nick."

As they stood together, her hand still in his, the predicted rain began to fall, fat drops splattering on the sidewalk. Mallory glanced at the parking lot as the breeze picked up and the shower began in earnest. "You're going to get wet."

Moving closer, he dropped her hand and cupped her cheek. "Not if I come inside."

She pulled her key out of her purse and unlocked the door. "Come in, then."

He followed her inside and shut the door. Behind them a brisk wind slapped rain against the door. He took her hand again, drew her toward him. "I want to stay."

She stepped into his arms. "I want you to stay." And then she kissed him.

Chapter Thirteen

Her kiss was tentative, a soft brush of her lips over his, but Kent felt it spread through his body like slow, sweet syrup. He kissed her back slowly to savor, to anticipate what he'd been longing for these many years.

But honor compelled him to lift his head. "Mallory, sweetheart, are you sure? The wine—"

Her laugh spilled out. "I asked myself that a few minutes ago. The answer was no. *Is* no. This isn't the wine talking, it's me."

"Thank God."

"Kiss me again," she murmured.

He did, thoroughly this time so if this were the only time, the last time, he wouldn't forget. But how could he? When he'd kissed her after the ball game the previous week, he'd learned that her flavor was the same, her scent hadn't changed and the soft sighs escaping her lips were echoes of those he'd heard the first time and all the other times they'd had together.

He raised his head, touched her swollen lips. "Mmm," she said. "More."

"In the bedroom," he answered, taking her shoulders to turn her around. She took his hand and led him into her room. It was dark, the only illumination from a night-light she must have gotten from Nick because it was shaped like a grinning frog.

He turned on the bedside lamp. "I want to see you." Forcing himself to go slowly, he unbuttoned her blouse and pushed it off her shoulders, reached behind her to unfasten her bra and helped her wriggle out of her enticingly tight jeans, then her lacy bikini panties.

Then he stood back and looked his fill. Her body was the same…yet different, too. A woman's body, more rounded, more…ripe. He cupped her breast and her breath caught, then he put his mouth to her nipple and she moaned.

Touching her nowhere but her breast, he drew her nipple deeper. Her hands clenched, fingers digging into his shoulders. "Kent," she panted, "you're… driving me…crazy."

"Driving myself crazy, too."

Mallory felt his laugh ripple against her chest. "Stop," she moaned again. "Let me…" She urged his head up, held him away and reached down to unfasten his belt. He wasn't the only one to tease and torment. She let her fingers skip playfully across his zipper and felt the bulge beneath grow larger, harder.

He pulled his shirt over his head and tossed it to the

floor, made quick work of his trousers and briefs, then reached for her again.

"Stop," she commanded, "let me look, too," and gazed at his aroused body. "You're beautiful," she said, raising her eyes to his.

"That's my line. You *are* beautiful, you know." Then he chuckled softly. "You're blushing all over."

He bent and reached into his pants pocket and unwrapped a condom. He'd brought protection. Of course. As soon as she'd opened her door to him, they'd both known how this night would end.

He opened the packet. So incredibly sexy, she thought, to see a fully aroused man, then watch him slowly sheathe himself.

And then he whispered, "Come here."

She did.

It had been so long, and now she was in his arms, his naked flesh against hers, his hot breath on her skin. While outside the rain beat against the window, he laid her on the bed. While thunder rumbled in the distance, he kissed and stroked her. When she could wait no longer and called for him, he parted her legs and entered her. Then he began to move and she met him stroke for stroke. More and more. Another and another. And then she fell apart in his arms. Seconds later he followed.

Later she snuggled against him, watching lightning streak through the sky, letting the rhythm of the rain lull her into a doze. She felt so safe, so serene here in his arms.

Kent kissed her temple. "Did I pass the test?"

"Hmm?"

"You said there'd be one after the movie."

Mallory giggled. "Honey, you aced it." She turned her head to grin up at him. "But there's a final exam." She pulled his head down and kissed him hard.

Kent groaned as her avid mouth met his, nipping, then soothing, then nipping once again. He tried to take control but this time she wouldn't let him. Her tongue swooped inside his mouth, stroked his tongue, enticing it to follow her lead.

She'd been like this as a young girl, he remembered hazily. He'd been her first lover, but she'd quickly learned to participate fully, to take the initiative. And she was doing it now.

Mallory loved being in charge. She straddled him, grinned and purred, "I have you where I want you now."

"You're a vixen."

"A what?" she laughed. "Did you get that from a Victorian novel?"

"From a dictionary. It means you're hot."

"I like that better." Mallory laughed, and then she froze, remembering. "D-do you have another condom?"

"Yeah, right here." He reached for his trousers. "Boy Scout. Always prepared."

Not always.

But she wouldn't think of the past now. She'd promised herself to live in the moment, and for the rest of this one night at least, she would.

Kent tore open the packet. "Let me," Mallory said and he handed her the condom. She spread it and slowly smoothed it over him. Cloaking him herself, stroking him as she did, was even more arousing than watching him do it.

And then she took him inside her. His warmth filled

her, completed her. This time she set the pace, fast and furious, a race to the finish. And later she fell asleep with her head on his shoulder and her hand in his.

It seemed she'd barely been asleep when the telephone rang. Mallory shot up and out of bed. This time the call had to be about Nick. Beside her, Kent sat up. She grabbed the phone, nearly dropping the receiver in her haste. "Hello."

"Mallory?" The voice was familiar but it wasn't Tamara's. Mallory was so unnerved she couldn't think who it might be.

"Yes, what's wrong?"

"Nothing, I hope. This is Karen."

Karen LeMay. "Oh, for God sakes, Karen. You scared me to death." She glanced at the clock on the bedside table. "It's nearly two o'clock. Is Steven all right? Do you need me to come over?"

"No, it's nothing like that," Karen answered. "I was worried about *you*."

"Me?"

Kent tapped her shoulder. "What's wrong?" he asked softly.

Mallory shrugged her shoulders. "I don't understand," she said to Karen.

Karen's voice lowered. "There's a car parked in front of your door. A black—no, it's a blue Honda. I saw it earlier, and when I got up to get a drink just now, it was still there."

Mallory rolled her eyes and stifled a giggle. "It's okay. I have company."

"Oh, I'm so relieved," Karen said.

"Thank you for calling." She put the phone down and fell backward on the bed, laughing.

Kent stared at her, a puzzled frown on his face. "What's going on?"

Still laughing, Mallory sat up and explained. "And the rumor mill will be in full gear tomorrow morning."

"Do you want me to leave?"

Mallory stopped laughing long enough to shake her head. "Absolutely not. I'm a grown woman. If I want to have 'company' in the middle of the night, it's okay." She propped herself up and ran a hand teasingly along his bare thigh. "Just wear a paper bag over your head when you leave in the morning."

And with that, they just had to make love again.

Mallory woke early to see sunlight filtering through the window and find Kent propped on his elbow, gazing down at her. "Hi." She rubbed his rough cheek. "Mmm, you look dashing in the morning."

He brushed the hair from her forehead. "I like waking up with you."

"That's nice."

His fingertip traced the line of her jaw. "I thought of this, of you through the years."

The mood spoiled for her, Mallory sat up abruptly and swung her legs over the side of the bed. "Don't! Don't bring up the past. Or the future. Don't say something we'll both be sorry for."

He put his hand on her shoulder, tried to urge her around to face him but she didn't move. "I don't understand."

She glanced over her shoulder at him. "Don't you?

We made love. It was great. Wonderful, in fact. You don't need to add pretty words."

"I didn't intend to." His face hardened. "Is that all this was for you, a one-night stand?"

She flinched. "No. It meant more than that." She moved farther away from him and scooped her bra and panties off the floor. "But I'm a grown woman now, Kent. What we had last night was enough. I don't need romantic words or promises you don't plan to keep."

"*I* don't plan to keep?" His jaw tensed, and he sat up on his side of the bed. "I'm not the one who didn't keep promises." Surprised at the bitterness of his words, she glanced over her shoulder as he added softly, "I've always wondered, Mallory. Why didn't you wait for me?"

Mallory yanked her shorts on, then turned to stare at him. "Did you expect me to wait until you finished your romantic tour of Europe?"

He looked as astonished as she felt. "My *what?*"

"Your vacation for two. You wanted me to wait in Valerosa like a sweet little small-town girl while you were traipsing all over Italy or...or wherever with some *woman.*" She didn't bother with her bra. She turned her back to him and began to fumble with the buttons of her blouse while her fingers shook.

"That's what you thought?" He got up and walked around the bed to stand in front of her with his hands on his hips. "Didn't Dr. Wilson call you and explain?"

"*Doctor* Wilson?" She tossed her head in disgust. "Wasn't that *Miss* Wilson? I called your hotel in Milan and they told me you and she had checked out. I thought they'd made a mistake on the name so I had them check again. They did. The person in the other room was *Clare*

Wilson, not Charles." Saying the words brought back all the hurt and humiliation she'd felt that long-ago morning, and she bit her lip to keep from letting more venomous words spew forth.

Kent sat down beside her heavily. "You really don't know what happened, do you?"

"Why don't you tell me?" And he'd better make it good, she thought as anger bubbled in her chest. She squeezed her feet into her sandals.

He waited until she was done with her shoes, then said, "Dr. Wilson—Dr. *Charles* Wilson—and I went to a medical conference in Milan. His daughter Clare was studying at the Sorbonne that year and she came to meet us in Milan. She and her father shared a room. I suppose the room was in her name because she got there first."

At least he didn't deny that there was a Clare Wilson. "Go on."

"We spent a lot of time together. In the evenings we did the city, the three of us. During the conference, Dr. Wilson ran into a former colleague who was living in Italy. He invited Charles to Palermo to give a talk to the staff at the hospital there. Charles wanted Clare and me to come along, so we left the conference a day early."

He paused and looked away, and suddenly the room was filled with a different sort of tension. "It's still hard to talk about," Kent muttered.

"What happened?" She needed to know but had a feeling she wouldn't like what she heard.

"We had a rental car. Clare was driving." His hands clenched in his lap. "We were on a winding road. We started around a curve so we were facing into the sun, and out of nowhere, we saw a car coming toward us, very fast. Clare tried to swerve but it was too late. We were hit head-on."

"Did the air bags—?"

"There were no air bags."

"My God." She put her hand on his arm.

He didn't acknowledge her touch, just kept talking. "Clare was killed instantly. So was the driver of the other car." Mallory gasped, but Kent continued talking. "Miraculously, Dr. Wilson came away with only a broken arm and a few cuts."

Mallory's hand tightened on his arm. "And you?"

"I had a broken collar bone and a head injury."

"Oh, Kent." She threw her arms around him and pulled him close. "H-how bad?"

"Pretty bad. I lost consciousness in the ambulance and didn't wake up for nearly three weeks."

"No," she whispered. Picturing Kent lying bruised and battered on the side of the road, she began to cry, sobbing softly against his chest. "No."

"Don't cry, hon. That was a long time ago." He stroked her hair. "Hey, I'm here now."

"I know, but—" She lifted her head and looked at him. "No one told me."

"I remember trying to tell Charles to call you when I was in the ambulance. Maybe I wasn't clear. Maybe he forgot. When I woke up, he was gone." He sighed. "He'd flown home with...with Clare."

Stunned, Mallory stared at him, then dropped her head into her hands as the implications of what he'd told her hit her full force.

Chapter Fourteen

"No. God, no," she moaned as tears flowed through her fingers.

Kent put his arm around her and hugged her close. "Don't cry for me, sweetheart. It's been over a long time."

She wasn't crying just for him, but for herself, for Nick, for Dean. But how could she tell Kent that?

Suddenly she lifted her head. "Let me see. I want to see where you were hurt."

"Mallory—" he began.

"Please."

"All right. He touched his head and she knelt beside him, carefully parted his dark hair and looked at the faint jagged line. Then she bent down and kissed it gently.

He reached for her and pulled her into his lap. "They had to shave my head."

"I bet you looked sexy."

He laughed. "I looked bald."

They sat silently for a few moments, holding each other tight, then Kent leaned back and looked into Mallory's eyes. "Why didn't you wait for me?" he asked.

"Because…" she began, and paused.

She didn't dare tell him the truth, not after all these weeks in Houston without saying a word.

Everything she'd done had been for Nick. All her dreams and hopes for her son hung on the next few words. His survival hung in the balance. She couldn't take a chance with Nick's life.

If she had to choose between doctor and father, Kent had to be Nick's doctor first and foremost.

"Because I thought you were with another woman."

"I understand how upset you must have been," Kent said softly, "but you married Dean so fast."

Puzzled, Mallory stared at him. "How did you know that?"

"I called you."

She gasped. "You called? When?"

"From Rome. As soon as I was awake and could get to a phone. I spoke to your housekeeper. She told me you'd gotten married a few days before."

Mallory's breath backed up in her lungs. If he'd called a couple of days earlier, he'd have been in time. But he hadn't. He *couldn't.* And her life—all their lives—had taken a different turn.

"Why?" Kent asked again. "I always knew Dean Brenner had a thing for you. I saw the way he looked at you. I never paid attention to how you looked at him because you said he was your buddy, your best friend. Was he more? Did you lead me on to make Dean jealous?"

"I—"

"Did you use me to egg him on to commit?"

Dear Lord, what could she say? If she said yes, she'd be admitting she betrayed Kent. If she said no, how did she explain her decision to marry Dean?

She decided to tell Kent part of the truth. The rest she'd keep hidden in her heart. At least until Nick was well. "I...I thought you weren't coming back."

"So you married Dean on the rebound."

"I suppose you could say that." If that's what he thought, so be it.

"The same reason I married Lisa," he muttered. "My marriage was a mistake. I picked someone who wasn't anything like you. I wanted to blot you out." He stroked her cheek. "But I couldn't."

"Kent, I don't know what to say."

"Just tell me one thing." He looked into her eyes. "Is there someone like Dean waiting for you now?"

That she could answer truthfully. "No. No one."

"Good." His lips curved in a lazy smile and he pulled her closer for a soft kiss that melted her bones. "Mmm, you taste delicious," he murmured.

"So do—"

The beep of his pager interrupted her words. With a sigh Kent eased her off his lap. He picked up his pants and found the pager in a pocket, checked the call-back number and reached for the phone.

Fascinated, Mallory watched as he instantly changed from lover to physician.

"Dr. Berger." He listened a moment, then said,

"Start the drip. I'm on my way." He hung up the phone and quickly began dressing. "Sorry," he said as he buttoned his shirt.

"Don't be. Someone needs you." Was it any wonder she wanted him to remain Nick's doctor? She walked him to the door, accepted his quick kiss and watched him hurry to his car.

When the sound of the Honda's motor died away, she curled up on the living room couch, shut her eyes and tried to digest all she'd heard this morning.

And all she'd said...or hadn't said.

One lie begets another. Was that one of her father's maxims? If not, it should be. Hers had been lies of omission, but falsehoods just the same.

Colossal mistimings had altered the course of her life. And the lives of all the people she cared about as well.

She remembered all too clearly the morning she'd called Kent's hotel and learned that he had gone.

She'd never imagined Kent would betray her this way. She'd never imagined she'd get pregnant, either. What was she going to do?

She'd sat, gazing into space, while tears rolled down her cheeks. Then the telephone had rung and she jumped up and grabbed the phone, certain it was Kent. But it wasn't. It was Dean.

"Could you come over here?" she asked tearfully.

"I'll be right there."

Her stomach began to roil as she put the phone down. She needed a drink of water. She stood and took one wobbly step toward the kitchen before the floor came up to meet her.

The next thing she knew she was lying on the

living room couch and Dean was kneeling beside her, a damp washcloth in his hand. "Is it the baby? Shall I call the doctor?"

Mallory shook her head and poured out the whole story of Kent's betrayal. Then she sat up. "He's a rat, Dean. He doesn't have the right to know about his child. I'll raise the baby by myself. I'll be a good mother, as good as two parents."

Dean sat beside her and regarded her thoughtfully. "If you're keeping this baby, you'll have to make a lot of plans."

"Yes, but the baby isn't due until late spring. I can go back to school." Suddenly her eyes filled with tears. "What am I going to tell my parents?"

He hesitated a moment, then said, "You don't have to tell them anything."

"Of course I do."

He put his arm around her. "No, you don't. Not if you marry me."

"Wh-what?"

"Marry me," he repeated.

Mallory stared at him. "I…can't." Seeing the hurt on his face, she rushed on. "*You* can't. I couldn't ask you to sacrifice your life for me. Don't you see, Dean? It would change all your plans, your whole life—"

"I know that. And it won't be a sacrifice. I love you, Mallory." He looked down at his hands, then up again. "I have for years."

Stunned, she gaped at him. "Years?" she mumbled. "You…you never said…"

"I thought you'd laugh. Your buddy in love with you."

He grasped her hands. "I'll make you happy, Mallory. And I'll be a good father to the baby."

"Kent's baby," she reminded him. "Wouldn't that always be on your mind?"

"It'll be *our* baby," he said firmly.

She could barely breathe. "I...I...don't know what to say...."

He tipped up her chin and kissed her very softly, very tenderly. "Say yes."

And so she did.

Her parents were stunned, especially when she told them she and Dean wanted to get married right away before Dean started classes at the University of Texas at El Paso.

"Isn't this rather sudden?" Lydia Roseman asked.

Her mother had a right to be puzzled, to ask questions. "Dean and I spent a lot of time together on the trip," Mallory answered, "and we realized we've cared for each other all along."

Lying wasn't easy, even though it was for her parents' sake as well as hers. How could her father stand in front of his congregation if his own daughter was an unmarried mother? How could her parents endure the gossip, the snickers about "the rabbi's daughter gone wrong"? How could *she?* But thanks to Dean, none of them would have to.

She wouldn't have the wedding of her dreams, with the long white dress, the veil, the bouquet of white orchids and lily of the valley. That was a small sacrifice.

And so, the following week they had the ceremony, with just their families and a few close friends present. Mallory wore a pink silk suit with a gardenia corsage.

Dean stood beneath the wedding canopy waiting for her, his eyes filled with love. When she reached his side, he took her hand in a warm, firm grasp. At the end of the ceremony when he performed the Jewish groom's tradition of stamping on a glass, the sound of glass breaking sounded so final, like the shattering of her dreams. But then Dean whispered, "I love you, Mallory." And when he kissed her, she promised herself she'd never think of Kent again.

Her long-standing friendship with Dean made the adjustment to marriage easier. As time went on, Mallory came to love him. When Nick was born, they became a family. And memories of Kent receded until they were only faint shadows in her mind.

And now Kent was back in her life. Now she knew the truth about his trip to Italy. She knew he'd begun to care for her all over again. But how could she think of a future with him? A future based on lies.

Chapter Fifteen

For most of the morning Mallory sat in the living room in a daze. *Accident…head injury…called you later…too late.* The words spun round and round in her mind until her head began to ache. She skipped breakfast, fixed herself a scrambled egg for lunch and choked down only half of it, then tried to write in her journal. The result was a mishmash of thoughts and emotions.

At two, Kent called and invited her to dinner at his house. She was torn between wanting to be with him and fearing the consequences of being with him too much. In the end, her heart won over her head. "All right. Give me directions and I'll drive myself." That would give her a measure of control. Besides, she wasn't as smug as she'd sounded this morning. She didn't want to feed the rumor mill at the apartment complex with a return of the blue Honda. Or more noticeably, the black Jaguar.

He told her how to find his house. "If you get here around five, we'll have time for a swim before dinner."

She concentrated on the pleasant evening they would have together and forced what she'd learned last night to the back of her mind. If she focused on the mistakes and regrets of the past, she might blurt out something and arouse Kent's suspicions. What had happened between them couldn't be undone. She'd put it behind her years ago and she would keep it that way. She'd continue to put Nick's needs first. And she'd allow herself to enjoy what she and Kent had together in the present and not think of the past. Or the future.

She hadn't brought a swimsuit to Houston so she drove back to the Rice Village shopping area where she'd bought Nick's baseball cap. There she found Just Add Water, a store with every kind of bathing suit anyone could imagine.

No bikini, no high-cut suit, just a plain one-piece, that's what she'd get. But not *so* plain that she looked like an old lady. She picked one with a swirl of colors—purples, reds, oranges. Perfect.

Her spirits lifted, she left the store and noticed a nail salon down the street. She'd treat herself to a manicure. Once in the salon, she decided on a pedicure, too. Why not? She'd planned to indulge herself this weekend.

Two chairs down from her a man was getting a pedicure. She'd never seen a man having his toenails done before.

Afterward she went to buy a bottle of wine for

dinner. Kent would probably grill hamburgers. She decided on a Merlot.

She found Kent's street easily and parked in front of his house, sat in the car for a few minutes and stared. His home was a clean-lined contemporary structure, large and obviously new. And intimidating. She was, after all, a small-town girl who rarely visited or even viewed such palatial homes.

Taking a breath to steady her nerves, she got out of the car. If they hadn't made love, if he hadn't told her about his accident, maybe she wouldn't be this tense. So much had changed since yesterday. *Don't think of it,* she reminded herself.

As soon as she rang the bell, Kent opened the door and drew her inside for a quick kiss. When she opened her eyes and got her breath back, she handed him the wine and looked around. The inside of his house was lovely, with a graceful staircase in the entry and wide windows in the living room facing a beautifully land-scaped lawn and a pool. Colors were neutral but the room was enlivened with paintings in bold hues.

This home might have been hers, she thought, if things had been different.

At one end of the living room was a grand piano and beside it a cello with a music stand in front of it. "Do you play?" she asked in surprise.

"I play a little but not well. I like old instruments," he said. "I have some more in the study." Something else she didn't know about him.

She changed in the guest bath and they took a quick dip in the pool, then sat beside it, holding hands and sipping margaritas.

Kent wore black-and-brown swim trunks. The first time she'd seen him by the pool in Valerosa, his swimsuit had been navy blue. He still looked as good as he had then. Mallory's eyes kept coming back to him, to the water droplets sparkling on his chest, to his tanned, muscular legs. To his toes, with neatly trimmed nails.

Such a deliciously sexy man. She wanted to lay her head on his chest and feel the sunlight against one cheek and his damp skin against the other. She wanted to rip off his swimsuit and hers and make love out here in the daylight. Good Lord, she was losing her mind.

Fortunately before she could act on her wicked thoughts, Kent excused himself to set out their dinner.

"Good grief," she said, staring in surprise at the patio table. She'd expected burgers; she'd gotten grilled salmon with fluffy rice pilaf and an array of grilled vegetables. She should have brought a Chardonnay. "How does a busy doctor have time to cook all this?" she asked.

"He goes to Central Market and buys dinner for two." When she gave him a puzzled frown, he added, "It's a superstore where you can buy any kind of food you can imagine."

"I'll have to try it out." She sipped her margarita. "Ah, if only Valerosa had a Central Market."

"Houston has a lot of things Valerosa lacks," Kent said. He didn't say any more. That was good because she couldn't handle any more just now. She knew he wasn't just talking about grocery stores.

After dinner she helped him with the dishes, then he took her hand and led her upstairs to his bedroom. The walls and carpet were white, the bedspread black and white in a geometric pattern. "Did your…wife decorate the house?" Mallory asked, pausing at the door.

"I bought this house after."

She was glad of that. She wasn't sure how she'd feel making love in the bed he'd shared with Lisa.

Thoughts of Lisa or any other woman he might have brought here fled as he eased her down to the bed. They undressed one another and made love slowly and deliciously, then bathed together in Kent's oversized whirlpool tub.

"You even have a towel warmer," Mallory said afterward as she wrapped a fluffy white towel around her. "My night of decadence."

Kent put his arms around her. "Come back in the bedroom and I'll show you decadence."

She followed him in. And he did.

Kent smiled down at Mallory snuggled against him in his king-size bed. She returned his smile, then yawned. "It's late. I should get home."

"Stay the night."

She shook her head. "I don't know what time Nick will be back tomorrow. It might be early."

"Call and ask."

She hesitated a moment, then said, "I'd really better go."

He let her, watching as she slipped out of bed and gathered her clothes, enjoying the sight of her pale backside as she leaned down to pull on her panties.

He got up and tugged on his briefs and jeans as she dressed quickly and fluffed out her hair. Arms around each other, they walked downstairs. At the door Mallory twined her arms about his neck. "Thanks for dinner. And dessert."

"Anytime." He kissed her deeply, not wanting to let her leave. "Wait. I'll get the car and follow you home," he offered.

She shook her head firmly. "I'll be fine." He started to protest and she added, "I'll call you the minute I'm home."

He let her go, watching as she walked to her car. When she drove away, he stood in the doorway, inhaling the fragrant night air, looking up at the ebony sky pinpointed with stars. He missed Mallory already.

Finally he turned, went back upstairs and dropped onto the bed to wait for her call. He could picture her here beside him in his bed night after night.

The one thing he couldn't seem to visualize was a wedding ring on her finger. Or one on his.

She'd hurt him once. He'd be a fool to let his heart propel him somewhere his head told him he wasn't sure he was ready to go. But when the phone rang and he heard her voice, he wondered if his heart was getting the upper hand.

The next afternoon when Nick returned, Mallory was sitting on the couch reading a paperback thriller. Her son came barreling in, beaming and chattering excitedly about his weekend adventures, the Spellmans' flat-screen TV and the pool table in their game room.

"Did you miss me?" Mallory teased.

"Mom, I'm not a *baby*. I've spent the night away before."

"I guess that means no."

"Yeah." He dragged his duffel bag into his room. "I'm hungry," he called.

Mallory followed him to his door. "I'll fix you a

sandwich, then you'd better get to bed before you fall over. We don't have an appointment tomorrow so you can sleep in."

She was glad they didn't have to go to the clinic in the morning. She wasn't sure how she'd react when Kent would be back in the role of doctor. And she didn't want Nick to pick up on any vibes between them.

Fortunately, they didn't see him when they were at the clinic on Tuesday. But he did call that evening just to talk. She lay in bed, listening to his voice and wishing he were beside her.

How would this end? She'd painted herself into a corner with Kent, and she wondered if she'd ever find a way to get out.

On Wednesday she found a message on her answering machine from a woman named Suzy Tucker. "I saw your story in the *Jewish-American Journal*," Ms. Tucker said, "and I wondered if you'd like to speak at the monthly meeting of the National Council of Jewish Women."

"Speak? Me?" Mallory squeaked after she'd listened to the message. Even thinking about talking to a group gave her stage fright. And what would she say? She decided to talk over the invitation with Tamara after the parents' weekly poker game.

She was late to the game. The children were at one end of the rec room working on a jigsaw puzzle they'd started a few days ago, the parents seated around a table at the other end.

The adults' talk and laughter stilled when Mallory walked in. Everyone stared at her. She stopped in the doorway and glanced down at her jeans and shirt. "What? Am I unzipped?"

A half laugh from Karen was the only response.

"Well, what is it?"

"Nothing," Karen said.

As Mallory sat down, Tamara admitted, "We were talking about you and Dr. Berger."

Of course. What else? "Yes?" Mallory said.

"We want the scoop. Are you and he 'together'?" Karen asked, fluffing her chestnut hair. Its rich brown color was compliments of a hairdresser, Mallory thought nastily.

"'Together' as in doctor and patient's mother? Yes. 'Together' as in man and woman? None of your business," Mallory said firmly. Someone laughed and she added, "We've known each other a long time, since long before he was Nick's doctor, so what's the big deal?"

"Sorry. We don't have much to do but talk," Naomi Peterson said. "We're just catty."

Weren't they just?

A sudden inspiration hit Mallory and she said, "Want something to do and something else to talk about? I have an idea." The other five women turned to listen. She told them about the message on her answering machine, then said, "Why don't we form a speakers' bureau? Everyone can contact their church or an organization of some kind and talk about bone marrow and stem cell donation. I'm scared silly of speaking in public, but if it helps Nick, I'll do it."

Interest dawned on their faces. "We could speak to birthing classes, talk about umbilical cord donation," Karen suggested.

The others chimed in. The poker game forgotten for the moment, they made plans. "I'll call the *Houston Chronicle*," Tamara said. "Maybe they'd do an article about us."

"Maybe Dr. Berger has a contact there," Mindy Nguyen said, and turned to Mallory.

"I'll ask," she said.

"My sister is a photographer here in Houston," Naomi said. "Maybe she could take some slides of the kids or make a video we can use when we give our talks." She laughed. "Listen to me. I'm talking like we're professional speakers."

"Maybe not professional, but we have a topic, so we can be speakers," Mallory said.

"I agree," Tamara said. "And we should name our group."

"Moms for Marrow," Mindy suggested.

"Something about cells," Karen said.

"Let's use Cells Equal Life Saving. That gives us an acronym—CELS," Naomi said.

"Perfect," Mallory said.

And when she told Kent about it on the phone that night, he agreed. "You're a great bunch of moms," he said.

"We are, aren't we? This will keep us occupied *and* keep our tongues from wagging."

"About what?"

"Blue Hondas." She laughed.

All the next week, working in the rose garden behind the apartment, taking Nick to appointments and back, writing in her journal, Mallory thought of what Kent had told her about his accident. As much as she'd told herself not to focus on the past, his words kept coming back to mind. Now that she understood why he hadn't kept his promise to come back to her, didn't she owe him the truth about Nick? In spite of her resolve to keep Nick's needs primary, her mind wavered back and forth.

Should she talk to him the next time they were together, lay everything out on the table, and hope he'd understand and forgive? Maybe this weekend—

But when she glanced at her date book, she realized that according to the Hebrew calendar, Saturday was the third anniversary of Dean's death. She and Nick would go to services on Friday night and again on Saturday morning. They hadn't attended synagogue since they'd been here. Perhaps this would get them back in the habit.

On Friday afternoon Mallory called Dean's parents. They reminisced about Dean, and she brought them up-to-date on Nick's progress.

That evening she lit the Sabbath candles, circling them with her hands three times, then covering her eyes as she said the blessing. She and Nick together said blessings over the bread and the wine—grape juice for Nick—and then she lit a memorial candle for Dean and said a prayer in remembrance of him. The smell of melting candle wax made her homesick, but as always, the Sabbath peace calmed her.

Later she and Nick went to services at Congregation Sinai, a nearby synagogue. She settled into her seat and realized she had missed the familiar music and prayers.

At the end of the service when Mallory rose to recite the mourner's prayer, Nick clutched her hand tightly. She glanced at him and saw that his eyes were bright with tears.

Afterward she took a few minutes to introduce herself

to the rabbi and to chat with several congregants, who welcomed her warmly, then she and Nick went home.

On the way he said, "Remember when Daddy used to play ball with me? I wish I could show him the baseball I got."

"He'd have loved it," Mallory said.

"He was a good dad."

She nodded, not trusting herself to speak over the lump in her throat. Dean had been a real father to Nick. He'd seen Nick take his first steps, taught him to swim and cheered him on at swim meets. He'd patiently drilled Nick on math facts and shared baseball lore. He'd seen Nick through a bee sting and a broken arm, bathed him when he had flu and fever. And so much more.

Later when Nick was asleep, Mallory curled up on the living room couch and gazed at the memorial candle that would continue to burn for twenty-four hours. *Such a small light for such a big person,* she thought, staring at the flame. Dean had been a good man, not just because he'd saved her life and Nick's. He'd been honest and honorable, hard-working and fun-loving. "I miss you," she whispered. "So does Nick."

All this time she'd wondered and worried about how Kent would react if he learned he was Nick's biological father. Until now she hadn't given much thought to Nick's reaction. How would her son respond to the truth about his parentage? What would he think and how would it affect his recovery if he found out that Dean, the man he loved and missed so much, wasn't his real father?

Chapter Sixteen

Mallory headed home from her speaking engagement, elated. Speaking in public, one of the major phobias of the human race and certainly hers, had not defeated her, she told herself proudly. Although her stomach churned all the way to the meeting and her legs threatened to give out under her as she walked to the podium, the speech had gone well. She'd told her audience about Nick, about their search for a transplant donor, and when she'd seen sympathy on the women's faces and tears in their eyes, she'd relaxed and spoken from her heart. At least half the women there had picked up flyers from the Bone Marrow Registry and several had come up to talk with her to learn more about the donation process. Now as she drove, she congratulated herself on the successful afternoon.

Before the meeting she'd looked up the location of Central Market, the source of Kent's fabulous dinner for two. She turned onto Westheimer and there it was. Smiling, she pulled into the parking lot. She'd treat the moms at the apartment to a celebration. This afternoon she might've saved a life. Not just Nick's, but another child's…other *children's* lives. Somewhere, one or more kids with leukemia would have a chance to grow up, get married, have children of their own.

She stepped inside the Central Market and stopped to stare, then wandered the aisles of the vast store. The temperature was chilly, but that hardly mattered. She'd entered a fantasyland of food. More kinds of bread than she'd ever seen, fresh produce, cheeses she'd never even heard of, teas and olive oils and mustards. The pungent smells of spices. The aroma of coffees.

She picked up sodas for the kids and a bottle of wine for the mothers, then a second. Why not have another celebration later with Kent? She added three cheeses and three kinds of crackers to her basket, then a dip and a pâté. Finally she grabbed a bag of popcorn for the kids.

As she strolled toward the check-out counters, she noticed an aisle of cake and cookie mixes, and stopped. Why not pick up a box and make a cake for Kent? She could never manage one from scratch but maybe she could deal with a box. She selected a mix for carrot cake and dropped it into her basket, then checked out. As she expected, when she arrived at the apartment, everyone was in the game room. "Success!" she called as she threw open the door. "Party time."

Applause sounded from the parents' table.

"Party time for us, too?" Jeremy Spellman asked.

"For everybody."

Soon the smell of popcorn permeated the room. Mallory poured the wine, and the parents raised their paper cups for a toast.

"*L'chaim*," Mallory said.

"What's that mean?" Mindy asked.

"To life."

The other moms echoed Mallory's words.

Giggling, the kids raised soda cans aloft in imitation. "Lime," Lori Nguyen said.

Nick fell back on the couch laughing. "Say it this way. Luh-hi-im. Got it?"

Lori tried without much success and a popcorn fight ensued. "Quiet down," Karen LeMay yelled in the voice of a drill sergeant. And finally, they did.

That evening Kent arrived home, opened his front door and heard the phone ringing. He sprinted to the bar and grabbed the receiver. "Hello."

"Hi." Mallory's voice.

He smiled and sat on a barstool. "Hi, yourself. How did your speech go?"

"Fantastic. Want to celebrate?"

"I'd like that. I'll pick up a bottle of wine."

"I already have some," she said. "I visited Central Market this afternoon. Why don't you come by around eight?"

"Blue Honda or black Jag?"

She laughed. "Let's confuse them. Bring the Jaguar."

"See you then." Smiling, he hung up. He'd had a hectic day, but talking to Mallory had erased all the small annoying incidents. Whistling, he pulled off his tie as he started upstairs. He shed his clothes, pulled on a pair of swim trunks and took a dip in his pool, then ate take-out Chinese at his kitchen table while he read a medical journal.

After a couple of articles, he closed the journal. Too distracted, too Mallory-starved. At the thought of seeing her, anticipation thrummed through his body. He knew, with Nick home, he and Mallory wouldn't make love tonight, but that didn't dim the excitement, the expectancy.

Precisely at eight, he rang Mallory's bell. Nick opened the door. "Hi, Dr. Berger. My mom's in the kitchen."

With Nick at his side chattering animatedly, Kent went to find Mallory. She stood at the kitchen counter, dressed in white shorts and a pink sleeveless top, her hair pulled into a ponytail. She didn't look much older than she'd been when they first met.

"Cooking?" he asked.

She turned to grin at him. "Arranging on a plate. Central Market is a noncook's dream come true."

Nick perched on a chair. "Did you know my mom gave a speech this afternoon?"

"I heard about it."

"And did you know she was scared silly? She said so."

Mallory's cheeks flushed. "Nick, that's a secret."

"Then the talk is really an accomplishment," Kent said. "Do you mind if I give your mother a hug to congratulate her?"

"Nah, go ahead. I won't look." Nick squeezed his eyes shut.

Kent stepped forward, put his arm around Mallory and hugged her gently. He felt the smoothness of her shoulder beneath his hand, inhaled her light, sexy perfume, and wanted to pull her flush against him and devour her.

And yet at the same time, he didn't need to. Being here in the brightly lit kitchen with her and Nick, knowing they'd spend the evening together, was enough.

His conflicting feelings confused him, and he stepped back, knowing he'd have to give some thought to this. "You can open your eyes, pal," he said, glancing at Nick with amusement.

"You two guys go have a seat," Mallory said. Kent noticed her cheeks were still pink. "I'll be there in a minute."

They sat at the breakfast table, talking about Mallory's afternoon, about the other women's ideas for snaring their own speaking engagements and making Cells Equal Life Saving a serious project.

"You know," Kent said thoughtfully, "if you really want to get your mothers group off the ground—"

"Of course we do."

"I mean long-term, after your own kids are well."

"Um, sure, I guess so," Mallory said hesitantly.

"Then there's someone you should meet. Her name's Veronica Mason. Her parents are substantial donors to the hospital, but Veronica's recently widowed and I know she wants to put together something in memory of her husband. I'm sure your group would interest her."

Mallory gaped at him. "You mean interest her in donating money?" When Kent nodded, she said, "Gosh, I wouldn't know what to tell her."

"What you first told me. She'd understand you're a fledgling organization, but she'd know how to help you

develop. I think that's what she's looking for." He
smiled at Mallory's stunned expression. "Want to give
it a shot?"

"Why not?"

"Okay, here's the bad news."

Mallory sighed. "Why shouldn't I have guessed
there'd be bad news, too?"

"There's a black-tie reception Thursday night—"

"This Thursday?" she squeaked.

"Yep, can you make it?"

"About as easily as I can fly," she answered. "Good
Lord, this calls for major planning."

"Go for it. I'll pick you up Thursday at eight."

"Okay."

Continuing their conversation, they discussed the
headlines of the day, then Nick's newest video game.
Kent was surprised at how relaxing the evening seemed
and how much he enjoyed just sitting here and talking.

Before Mallory and Nick, his social life had been
more sophisticated. He'd enjoyed evenings at the opera
or symphony or the city's best restaurants with glamor-
ous women on his arm, but the pleasures had been short-
lived. This was different.

As he pondered the difference, Mallory got up to
clear the table. Kent was halfway out of his seat when
she said, "Stay. Nick will help me."

Kent's eyes followed her admiringly as she gathered
their plates and left the room. Maybe he'd taken the next
step, he thought, beyond just *wanting* her, to wanting to
be *with* her. Maybe the seed of trust was showing its first
tiny sprout.

But he wouldn't rush headfirst into a long-term

relationship the way he had before. He was older now, more experienced. They'd spend time together, and this time around, he'd be sure before making a serious move.

Later, after he told Nick good night, Mallory walked him to the door and put her hand on his arm. "I want to ask you something," she said quietly.

Her expression had turned serious. This must be a question about Nick. "Okay."

"We haven't heard anything from the bone marrow registry. I'm worried."

He wasn't surprised at the question. She'd spent the day soliciting donors. How could she help thinking about her own child's needs? He put his hand over hers. "It's only been a few weeks."

"Only?"

"In bone marrow terms, a few weeks equals a very short time."

"Isn't there some other way—?"

He shook his head. "All I can say is, 'Be patient.' Look, why not get away for a couple of days? This weekend I'm on call but we could go somewhere the next one."

"I can't 'get away,' Kent. I've told you before, the leukemia's always with me."

"I know." He stood quietly, pressing her hand, wishing he could perform a medical miracle and make Nick's illness disappear.

Mallory let out a breath. "What kind of getaway were you thinking of?" she asked.

"Cedar Shores Resort at Lake Travis, near Austin. Why don't we spend the weekend there?"

She pulled away. "I can't leave Nick."

"I meant *with* Nick." He felt her fingers tighten under

his hand and before she could object, added, "We'll get separate cabins."

Her smile was slow, tentative, but she said, "All right."

"Great. I'll make the reservations."

"Fine, but I'll pay for my own room," she said firmly.

"Deal."

As he stepped out the door, she said, "You're very persuasive. You've talked me into a lot this week."

He laughed. "Trust me, I'll talk you into more." He touched her cheek and headed for his car.

Did he want to talk her into more? He wasn't at all certain. Maybe the next weekend—two uninterrupted days with her and Nick—would help him decide.

The next morning, Mallory called Karen to tell her about the black-tie reception. "I need help," she said. "I don't have anything to wear."

"Fashionista squad to the rescue," Karen said. "Tamara and I will be there in fifteen minutes."

When Mallory opened the door, they marched into her apartment. "Closet search first," Karen announced.

They followed her into the bedroom. "Okay," Tamara began, "first we have to—" She gaped at the dresser where a baking pan filled with batter sat. "What's that?"

Mallory shrugged. "I was going make a cake for Dr. Berger last night, but I couldn't, so I hid it."

"Why couldn't you bake it?" Tamara asked. "It looks ready to go in the oven."

"Well, that was the problem. I don't know which kind my oven is." Her friends looked puzzled, and she went on. "There were two sets of directions on the box, one for low altitude and one for high. I didn't know which to use."

"Low," Tamara said. "Houston's at sea level."

"Is that what the directions mean? I thought it meant top oven or bottom one. There's only one oven in the kitchen here so I didn't know which altitude it was."

Karen and Tamara looked at each other, then began to giggle. Shaking with laughter, Tamara flopped down on the bed. "Mallory, haven't you ever baked a cake before?"

Flushing, Mallory shook her head.

"Don't. You obviously aren't cut out for cooking."

"Never said I was," Mallory mumbled, then laughed, too. "Once I made a zucchini casserole with cucumbers."

Karen held her sides. "I believe it. Thank goodness you didn't ask us over here to give you a cooking lesson. You're beyond help, so let's hit the closet."

After searching through the meager wardrobe Mallory had brought to Houston, they all agreed the black-tie reception called for a major shopping expedition. Leaving the kids with Tamara that afternoon Mallory and Karen headed for the Galleria. They rushed, then walked, then trudged through the Galleria until Mallory found the perfect dress, shoes whose sexiness belied their comfort and an evening bag to match.

Thursday evening the moms assembled at Mallory's apartment to help her get ready. Mindy did her hair in a sleek chignon held in place by a tortoiseshell clip. At the last minute Tamara released a few tendrils to frame Mallory's face.

Karen did her makeup. "This is like a sorority house on Saturday night," she said.

"You all are so nice to do this for me," Mallory said.

"Hey, you're our representative at this bash. We want you to make a good impression," Karen said.

"And now, ladies, let's get outta here before the fraternity hunk shows up."

The kids were watching the Cartoon Network in the living room. When Mallory came in, Nick looked up. "Wow, Mom, you look like a movie star."

"My hero." Mallory dropped a kiss on his cheek, which he immediately and pointedly wiped off.

As the mothers and children headed for the door, Tamara said, "Come on, Nick. You're staying with us."

"Mom, can't I wait and say hi to Dr. Berger?"

"Okay, then we'll walk you to Jeremy's."

A few minutes later when the doorbell rang, Mallory scooted back into the bedroom to take one last glance in the mirror, then went to open the door.

Kent stared. She stood in the doorway, framed by the living room light. She wore a stunning ankle-length dress of bronze, shot through with gold threads. Tiny straps over her shoulders begged to be slipped down to give access to the smooth skin beneath. The bodice was cut low enough to draw his eyes to her cleavage. No necklace hid her slender neck or competed for attention with the teasing view of the tops of her breasts. The dress's slinky material clung to her body, caressing soft curves. A bold slash in the gently flared skirt provided a tantalizing view of one slim leg from ankle to thigh. High-heeled sandals matched the dress and accented the length of her legs. Her only jewelry was a pair of bronze earrings that nearly skimmed her delectable shoulders.

Mallory's welcoming smile turned tentative. "Is this all right?"

Kent cleared his throat. "I'm speechless."

"Really?"

He nodded. "You're...beautiful."

She glanced away, then back. "Thank you."

"Shall we?"

She glanced behind her. "Nick, didn't you want to say hello to Dr. Berger?"

"Yeah...yes." Nick appeared at Mallory's side. "Hi."

Kent tore his eyes from Mallory to focus on her son. "Hi," he said.

"Scoot, Nick. We'll watch you walk to the Spellmans'," Mallory said. Nick galloped down the walkway, then turned and waved.

From the table by the door Mallory picked up a tiny beaded bag that Kent thought was surely too small to hold more than a tissue, and they were on their way in Kent's Jaguar.

"Tell me more about Veronica Mason," Mallory said as they turned onto the street.

"She comes from oil money. Her father owns one of the biggest independent oil companies in Texas. Gerald Maroney." He glanced at Mallory, then quickly back to the road. Her fragrance filled his nostrils. She smelled of sultry summer days, lazy moonlit evenings...

He braked at a red light.

"Even out in the sticks I've heard of Gerald Maroney," Mallory said. "He's a legendary character."

"Veronica's mother's family were cattle ranchers." He glanced over at Mallory. The sight of her bare leg inches from his made his hand itch to leave the steering wheel, to travel along that smooth skin...

A honk from behind them jarred him back to attention, and he drove forward along the freeway feeder. The driver in back of him sped by them up the ramp, emphasizing his impatience with another loud and lengthy honk as he went past.

"And Veronica?"

"Hmm?" He'd been imagining ending his journey at Mallory's hips, sliding her panties down and kneeling before her to feast his hungry mouth on her tenderest parts. Voice hoarse, he said, "She's a *grande dame*—board of the opera, the Museum of Fine Arts, the Alley Theater. Her husband was…"

Mallory turned toward him, setting the long columns at her ears to swaying. He cleared his throat. "He was—" damn, he was too distracted to remember "—a, um…criminal attorney." Yeah, that was right. "High profile."

"Sounds like an intimidating family," Mallory said. "I'm getting butterflies."

"You can handle her. I've laid the groundwork. Just be yourself."

"The rabbi's daughter from Nowhere, Texas."

He thought for a moment that she was joking, then he turned his head and saw her nervous fingers clasping and unclasping her bag. He took her cold hand, brought it to his lips. "You'll do fine."

"I'll picture her in her underwear."

He chuckled and pictured Mallory in hers.

Chapter Seventeen

Kent listened as Mallory chatted with Veronica Mason. The two had quickly discovered a common love of gardening. As Mallory told Veronica about the rose garden she'd planted behind the apartment and how each child had chosen a bush, the older woman listened with interest. "What a splendid idea," she said.

Kent was surprised to learn that Veronica raised orchids. She described her latest exotic variety and said to Mallory, "You must come and visit someday and see the gardens. You, too, Kent."

"I'd like that." He would. He found Veronica both charming and challenging. In her mid-sixties, she was as slim and toned, had as flat a stomach as a woman thirty years her junior. Like Mallory's, her hair was pulled back in a smooth chignon; unlike Mallory's, it was tinged with silver.

In contrast to her youthful body, Veronica's face was lined. She was said to disdain cosmetic surgery and was often quoted as remarking to a contemporary that money spent on erasing lines that would only come back was no better than money flushed down the toilet. "I've got creases on my face from experience," Kent had once heard her say, "and I see no reason to make some hotshot surgeon rich by trying to hide them."

Recent tragedy had added new, deeper lines. Veronica's husband, a vigorous man, had died in the crash of a private plane, the only fatality on board.

Kent's pager sounded and he excused himself and stepped away from the crowd to return the call. One of his hospitalized patients was complaining of pain. He gave the order for medication and asked the nurse to call him back in two hours to let him know how the child was doing.

Slipping his cell phone back into his pocket, he stood watching Mallory from across the room. Several other people had joined her and Veronica, but Kent had eyes for Mallory alone. In the circle of beautifully coiffed and designer-gowned women she stood out like a beacon. She was unaffected and enthusiastic. And alluring.

He felt his body heat, felt himself harden. The desire she'd sparked during their drive over here burst into a flame so fervid he felt like a lust-driven teenager, but he couldn't seem to help himself. He wanted to march across the room and carry her off like some prehistoric caveman.

"Kent."

He jumped at the male voice behind him. He turned and saw William Fleming, a cardiologist. "William, how's it going? Haven't seen you for a while," he said, extending his hand. He and William belonged to the same health club. He wondered if his friend noticed the evidence of how very healthy Kent was feeling at the moment.

They talked for a few minutes, Kent finding it difficult to keep his mind on the conversation while Mallory filled his mind, and desire warred with politeness. He willed his body to relax, and finally it obeyed.

After a while, he excused himself and headed back to Mallory. Others had joined her group while he was gone, and the conversation ranged from the latest appointment to the federal judiciary to the new conductor who was to take over the Houston Symphony in the fall. Drinks and hors d'oeuvres were passed by tuxedo-clad waiters, and the conversation continued to flow. Finally Veronica said, "I really must go. I have an early appointment with my dentist." She grimaced. "Not my favorite way to begin the day. Mallory, I'll call you and perhaps we can get together next week."

Perfect timing, Kent thought as Veronica started toward the door. He glanced at his watch. "How about you?" he said to Mallory. "Ready to go?"

She nodded, they said their goodbyes, and he took her arm and steered her toward the exit. As they moved through the crowd, several people greeted them and each time they had to stop to chat. And each time Kent's tension level zoomed higher. But after what seemed like forever, they made their way out of the ballroom and into the hallway.

"This was a wonderful evening," Mallory said. "Thank you."

Her eyes sparkled and again, her smile went straight

to his loins. He jabbed the elevator button, punched it again. A small sign on one of the two elevators said Out of Service, but he heard the motor as the other car moved toward their floor. *Thank God.*

"In a hurry?" Mallory asked.

"Damn right," he muttered as the doors slid open.

Puzzled, Mallory frowned as Kent all but dragged her inside the elevator. Tension seemed to emanate from him. His jaw was clenched, his expression unreadable. "Kent?" she asked. "Is something wrong?"

"No...yes. Dammit, I need to touch you."

"Oh," she murmured. "I—"

She had no chance to finish. Kent pulled her into his arms, crushing her against him. Then his mouth was on hers.

His kiss was ravenous. Against her chest his heart pounded frantically. He reached behind him, jabbed at the stop button and the elevator shuddered to a halt.

He pushed her back against the elevator wall. She felt the cool metal against her back, the heat of Kent's body against her. And everything disappeared but him. All thoughts vanished from her mind. All that mattered was him, his avid mouth racing across her face, teeth nipping her lips, his breath rasping in her ear. She moaned, kissed him back, sucking at his tongue, flicking her tongue over it while her hands searched for exposed flesh to touch, to taunt.

He pulled the strap off one of her shoulders and kissed his way down to the upper curve of her breast. Impatiently he pushed aside the silky material of her bodice. She wore no bra and, groaning, he filled his hand with her naked breast. His lips followed, scorching a path to her nipple while one hand pushed her skirt out of the way and caressed her thigh. Oh, God, this was torture, this was heaven.

With his other hand, he struggled with his zipper.

A loud beep stilled his hand. Someone was calling for the elevator.

"The other's…out of service," she gasped.

Panting, they broke apart. Kent disengaged the stop button and the elevator started down. "Just as well," he said hoarsely. "No condom."

Mallory let out a breath. Thank God someone wanted the elevator. She knew only too well the capability of Kent's sperm.

Still leaning against the wall, Mallory pulled up the bodice of her dress, smoothed her hair. Beside her Kent straightened his tie. His hands shook.

With a slight bump, the elevator came to a stop.

Mallory glanced at Kent. His zipper was still undone. As the door began to open and she saw an elderly couple standing before them, she stepped in front of him. "Zipper," she said under her breath.

"Party over?" the gray-haired man asked.

Ours is.

"Still in full swing," Kent said, following Mallory out, and the couple moved around them and into the elevator.

The downstairs hallway was empty, but outside the door stood several valet parking attendants. Kent faced the wall, pulled up his zipper and turned around.

Still breathless, Mallory patted her hair again. "I bet we looked guilty." A laugh bubbled up, and she couldn't control it. "They…almost…caught us," she giggled. "We would've looked…like…like horny teenagers."

Burying her face in Kent's shoulder she laughed until she had no breath left, until tears filled her eyes.

When she lifted her head, she saw that Kent had been laughing, too. Wiping his eyes with his hand, he said with a trace of laughter still in his voice, "Adventure over. We're grown-ups now."

At the door he handed the attendant his parking stub, and they stood waiting. Each time their eyes met, they chuckled.

And then their car arrived. They got in, and with a rumble of the Jaguar's powerful motor, they were on their way home.

Fifteen minutes later, hoping she didn't look too disheveled, Mallory knocked softly at the Spellmans' door. Tamara opened it and put her finger to her lips. "I got the boys to sleep about half an hour ago," she whispered.

Inside, Mallory saw Nick sprawled on the couch, one arm hanging over the edge. On the floor beneath his hand lay a Marvel comic book. She went to him. "Nick," she said, "wake up, sweetie. It's time to go."

Nick muttered something but his eyes didn't open. "Nick," Mallory repeated and put a hand on his cheek, then jerked it away. "He's warm."

Kent came to her side, touched Nick's forehead. "You're right." He lifted Nick in his arms. "Let's go home. We'll take his temperature and you can change, in case—"

"In case what?"

"In case he needs to go to the hospital," Kent said matter-of-factly.

Mallory's heart jumped. Not again.

"He was fine an hour ago," Tamara said, frowning.

"You know these kids. A fever can spike in minutes," Kent said.

Tamara caught Mallory's hand as she started out the door.

"Call and let me know."

"I will." She squeezed her friend's hand and followed Kent.

In her apartment he laid Nick on his bed. Mallory handed him the thermometer.

"Hey, pal, it's Dr. Berger. Open up."

Nick obediently opened his mouth. His eyes were glazed.

Without waiting for the temperature reading, Mallory knew they'd have to go to the hospital. She hurried into her bedroom, pulled off her evening clothes and without bothering to hang up the dress, grabbed a pair of jeans and a T-shirt. She tossed her sandals on the floor, changed into tennis shoes and socks, then went back to Nick's room. "How high?"

"A hundred and three."

"I have some Tylenol in the bathroom."

"Not now. Not until we know what's wrong." Kent lifted Nick again. "Okay, Nick, we're going for a ride."

"Yeah," the boy muttered. His head lolled on Kent's shoulder.

They entered the hospital through the emergency room. While Mallory went through the admissions process, Kent carried Nick back to a cubicle. A resident followed.

Mallory watched them over her shoulder as the admissions clerk photocopied their insurance card, then recorded Nick's hospital number, date of birth, symptoms. It seemed he wrote in slow motion. Why did they have to go through this same process every time they entered the hospital? Surely Nick's records were on file. Finally, the bored-looking man finished and Mallory hurried to find Nick.

He looked wan and small lying on the examining table. "Mom?" he said, his eyes suddenly opening. "Is this the hospital?"

She took his hand. "Yes."

"What're we doin' here?"

"You're running some fever." She glanced at Kent.

"A hundred and four," he told her.

Mallory felt a sweat break out. It seemed a long time ago that she and Kent had been locked in a passionate embrace. They'd spent a few hours in a fairy-tale world. This was her real life.

"I've listened to his chest," Kent continued, "and he sounds a little raspy. I've ordered a chest x-ray."

Without letting go of her son's hand, Mallory pulled a chair closer to him. Within minutes an attendant appeared with a wheelchair. Mallory walked beside Nick as he was pushed to the x-ray room.

Kent went inside with him. "Stay here," he said. "It'll only take a few minutes."

As promised, ten minutes later he emerged from the room. He took Mallory's hand. "We're going to admit him," he said. "He has pneumonia."

Chapter Eighteen

An electric shock surged through Mallory's body. "B-but he's been in remission. Does this mean the cancer's come back?"

Kent took her icy hand in his. "No," he said firmly. "This doesn't mean a recurrence of cancer. Not at all."

"What, then?"

"He's got some fluid in his chest." He dropped her hand and urged her out of the cubicle.

Ahead of them two men in scrubs guided the stretcher on which Nick lay. Mallory quickened her pace to walk alongside her son. "Why?" she asked, turning to Kent.

He shook his head. "I—"

"Don't know," she finished for him. Shock had given way to anger and despair. "You're going to tell me 'these things happen.'"

"Yes, they do." Frustration showed in Kent's voice, too. "Nick's immune system is weak. This is not uncommon." He reached toward her, then as if remembering where they were, dropped his hand. "I've ordered antibiotics. The nurse will start them as soon as Nick's in a room."

Mallory's fists clenched. "How long until the antibiotics work?"

"Soon."

The staff elevator doors opened. Kent and Mallory followed as the orderlies pushed Nick's stretcher inside. The doors slid shut and Mallory squeezed her hands tighter. This was a very different elevator than the one she and Kent had shared earlier. Different emotions now. Fear, anger. She wanted to stamp her foot. She wanted to yell at God: *Why are you doing this to an innocent child?* No use. Her father, ever the rabbi, would answer with the title of a book written by another rabbi, that sometimes bad things happen to good people. She sighed. "How long will Nick be in the hospital?"

Kent spread his hands. "Again, I don't know. Probably a few days."

In the hospital room Nick was transferred to a bed. Mallory sank down on the lounge chair in the corner of the room. A young nurse entered, introduced herself, took vital signs, then efficiently hung a bag of liquid and started it dripping into an IV line in Nick's arm. "That chair turns into a bed," she told Mallory. "If you're going to spend the night, I'll bring some linen."

"Just a blanket," Mallory said. Suddenly she was exhausted, but she knew she wouldn't sleep.

In a few minutes the nurse returned with a light

blanket. "Thanks," Mallory said. She laid the folded blanket in her lap, not sure what she wanted to do with it.

A worried frown on his face, Kent said, "You should try to get some sleep." He took the blanket from her limp hands and gently spread it over her, then leaned against the window ledge, watching her.

Mallory managed a half smile. "You need sleep, too," she told him. "I'm sure you have a full day tomorrow." He nodded but said nothing, and she said firmly, "Don't stay, Kent. Go home. If I need you, I'll call." Suddenly it seemed vitally important to her that she face this night alone.

"All right." He went to the bed for a last look at Nick, then came back to Mallory. He bent and dropped a kiss on her forehead. "Sleep," he murmured and left.

Through the night Mallory never shut her eyes. She read and reread the numbers on the monitor by Nick's bed, watched the movements of his chest, and got up now and then to put her hand on his forehead. The nurse slipped in and out, checking vital signs, removing bags, hanging new ones. Near morning someone from the lab came to draw blood. Nick slept through it all.

By the middle of the next day the antibiotic had begun working, and Nick's next chest x-ray showed improvement. But not enough. Another day in the hospital.

Mallory's thoughts jumped from one question to another. The last antibiotic had worked faster. Did this mean he was becoming resistant to them?

If Nick had a transplant right away, would he still have to go through these "episodes"? What if she just blurted out to Kent that he was Nick's father? No matter how Kent felt about that, he'd agree to be screened. Maybe they could hurry the process, maybe he'd be a match. "If we find a donor," she said to the nurse, "then Nick won't have to suffer with infections or pneumonia anymore."

The young woman shook her head. "Transplant patients are still prone to these setbacks. More than half end up in the hospital posttransplant."

Mallory's heart sank. She'd wanted confirmation of her idea, wanted to believe there was an end in sight to this nightmare. When the nurse left, she stared out the window at the summer sky. No use telling Kent.

One day in the hospital stretched into two, then four. Nick was awake enough to be testy. Bored with TV, uninterested in his Game Boy, he pouted and whined, pushing all of Mallory's buttons. That, coupled with her own anxiety, made the days almost too much to bear.

On day five Kent said, "Things are looking up. If everything's all right in the morning, we'll send you home."

"Sweet," Nick said and inwardly Mallory echoed the word.

Kent beckoned to her and she followed him into the hall. "How are you holding up, Mom?" he asked. "Getting any sleep?"

"A little."

"Not enough." Gently, he traced a circle under her eye.

"I'll be better when we're home," she said.

"You're tired. What else is going on?" Kent asked.

She sighed bitterly. "You know how I feel? Like I'm one of those pioneer women who set out across the prairie. When they get where they're going, the family builds a farm and plants crops, and then a tornado comes and knocks down the house, one of the kids gets gored by a bull, and the corn gets infested by some sort of insect so the crop fails. And *she* just keeps on keepin' on."

"And so do you. You're a strong woman, Mallory."

She'd heard those words before. "Dr. Sanders said the same thing."

"He's right," Kent said. "You'll get through this. The pneumonia is just a bump on the road."

"I'll try to remember that," she said and hoped she could.

The Sunday after Nick left the hospital, Veronica Mason invited Mallory and Kent for lunch. To Nick's disgust, Mallory decided she'd imposed too much on Tamara Spellman and hired a sitter from the list given out by the clinic. When the sitter rang the doorbell, Nick stomped to the couch and sat on one end, arms crossed on his chest.

"Stop glowering," Mallory warned.

"I don't even know what that means."

"Frowning, scowling. New vocabulary word."

Nick stuck out his lower lip and said nothing.

"Behave yourself. I mean it."

Mallory opened the door to a pleasant-looking, gray-haired woman.

Kent was right behind the sitter. He wore khakis and a navy blue polo shirt and looked as sexy as he had in a tuxedo a week ago.

Mallory gave the sitter instructions and with one last pointed look at Nick, left the apartment. Kent turned on the CD player in the car and Mallory leaned back and relaxed for the first time in days.

Veronica's house was in the posh River Oaks section

of Houston, where money fairly dripped from the trees. It was a white antebellum structure with graceful columns set back on a wide expanse of green lawn lined with azalea bushes. In the spring the yard must be breathtaking, Mallory thought as they got out of the car.

Veronica opened the door herself. Today she wore cream-colored silk pants and a long-sleeved turquoise blouse. Again, her hair was pulled back in a bun. She ushered them into a sunroom where a glass-topped table was set with five places. The windows looked out on a backyard that was even more impressive than the front. Even Mallory, who prided herself on her knowledge of horticulture, couldn't recognize all the plants.

Veronica introduced her son, Grant, and her daughter, Claire Humphreys. They made small talk, then Veronica asked, "Would you like to see my orchids?"

She led them out the back door to a greenhouse. Inside, the humidity soared, but Mallory hardly noticed. This was an orchid lover's dream. Naming the varieties—Lady of the Night, Cattleya, Lady's Slipper—Veronica led them past plants with blooms of almost translucent white, deep purple, yellow. "Here's my newest addition," she said, pausing before a dazzling white flower with a reddish-blue center. "It's a pansy orchid. They're very hard to grow."

"Orchids are Mom's passion," Claire said, giving her mother a fond look. "She could supply a whole schoolful of senior prom corsages."

"And waste my babies on unappreciative teenagers?" Veronica sniffed. "Not a chance."

They strolled back inside the house and sat down to salads of thick ripe tomatoes, fresh asparagus, hearts of palm and capers on dark green lettuce leaves.

"I'm not one to waste time," Veronica said briskly, setting her fork down. "Mallory, I've spoken to Grant and Claire about your ideas and they're interested."

"Very," Claire agreed. "I think Dad would be pleased to have his name associated with an organization dedicated to helping children."

Mallory's heart began to pound. "We're not quite far along enough to be called an organization," she said.

"But you will be. Meanwhile we need a proposal—your name, mission, how you intend to accomplish it."

Mallory swallowed. "All right. How soon?"

"A month," Grant said.

"You'll have it," Mallory answered with a great deal more confidence than she felt.

They continued talking, and she glanced across the table at Kent to find his eyes on her. Her mind flashed to the last time she'd talked with Veronica—the reception and the elevator ride afterward—and she felt her cheeks flush. Quickly, she looked away.

They left after brunch, and on the way home Kent suggested they make another reservation at Cedar Shores. They'd had to cancel their rooms, of course, when Nick had taken sick, but with the resilience of childhood, Nick had bounced back from his illness and was now himself again.

"I'm sure Nick would love to go," Mallory said.

"And you?"

"Me, too."

"Good. I'll call as soon as I get home. They're not likely to be crowded. School's already started in lots of places."

School. Somehow the summer had passed without

Mallory's realizing it. Soon the first crisp days of autumn would arrive. In Valerosa, Nick's friends would be back at their desks, grumbling about homework, playing fall football. Sadly, she compared their lives with Nick's. Needles, doctors, chemo.

When would this ever end?

She could almost hear her father's words. *Don't think about that. Enjoy the moment.* All right, she would. They'd have a carefree weekend. She'd focus on that.

"Make the reservations," she told Kent. "In the meantime, I have things to do. I have to talk to the others in our group and see if they want to tackle this proposal. After all, they're busy. Every one of them is a caregiver for a sick child."

"So are you," Kent pointed out as he steered the Jaguar out of River Oaks and onto Kirby Drive. "Do you *want* to get this organization going?"

"Yes," she answered firmly. "And I think the rest of the moms will, too. It's a chance to help kids, not just ours but maybe hundreds of others. How can we pass this up?" She stretched her legs. "I almost fainted when Veronica started talking about proposals and mission statements. What do I know about that kind of stuff?"

"I'll get you together with Sandy Worrel, the fund development person at the hospital," Kent said. "She can give you some tips."

"Thanks. You're my hero."

He grinned and laid a hand on her thigh. "Want to prove it?" Slowly, he moved his fingers higher.

Mallory shivered but swatted his hand away. "You wish."

* * *

After meeting with Sandy, Mallory talked to the rest of the moms. As usual, they gathered around the card table in the apartment rec room. Potato chips and dips from a nearby grocery were at hand.

"We need a fund-raising strategy," Tamara said. "Something that will…define us."

"Something easy and catchy," Mindy added.

"Yeah," Karen, who rarely missed a chance to give an opinion, said. "Look what the Susan B. Komen Foundation has done with their Race for the Cure."

"Or Lance Armstrong's yellow bracelets," Naomi chimed in as she reached for more chips. "He started a national fad."

"So we don't want to copy him," Tamara said. "How about having kids take little bags along when they go trick-or-treating? The bags could say Coins for Kids."

"Or," Mallory suggested, "we could sell red roses for Mother's Day. What's a better present for a mother than a child's life?"

"Great," Tamara said. "We could even use a red rosebud as a logo."

"I like that, but let's list several suggestions," Karen said, "and see what the Mason family likes. We can work on our mission statement over this weekend."

Mallory glanced down at her soda can. "I'll be gone."

"Where to?" Karen asked.

Mallory felt her cheeks heat. "Um, Cedar Shores Resort in Austin."

"And not alone, I bet," Karen said with an arch smile.

Mallory smiled back but didn't answer.

Chapter Nineteen

The hills west of Austin, still summer-green, were a welcome change from Houston's flatness. Mallory was glad Kent had suggested this getaway. It was nice to leave the city behind, she thought, and stared lazily out the window as they drove along Lake Travis, its blue water reflecting the sky. And when they drove through the gate of Cedar Shores, she knew he'd chosen the perfect spot.

At first sight, the resort looked like a picture from a glossy travel magazine, or the way she imagined a vacation spot in the Alps might look. Only these weren't mountains in the background; they were barely high enough to be called hills.

Kent drove up to the main building with its wide windows and large patio. When they got out of the car,

Mallory could see cabins built of stone nestled among aromatic cedars and massive oaks.

After registering and putting away their clothes in their adjoining cabins, they explored the area, meandering along well-trodden paths. As they strayed farther into the woods, Mallory whispered, "Shh," and pointed ahead. A doe stood in a small clearing, her fawn beside her.

"Wow," Nick whispered.

As they stopped to watch, the doe caught their scent and bounded gracefully away with her fawn following.

Kent led them along a path down to the shore of the lake where a fishing pier enticed anglers and a dock offered space for a collection of sailboats and motorboats. Farther down the shore was a swimming area, and back near the main building an Olympic-size pool beckoned.

"Can we go swimming?" Nick asked.

"Not a good idea," Kent said firmly, "but we can rent a boat or sit on the pier and fish."

"Fish," Nick said, then wondered, "If we catch any, what will we do with them?"

"Take them to the kitchen," Mallory said.

"You'll cook them?"

"No, the resort kitchen," she said. "This is a vacation. No cleaning fish, no cooking."

They wandered back past tennis courts, shuffleboard courts and a nine-hole golf course. "The main building has a spa and two movie theaters," Kent said.

"Do you come here often?" Mallory asked, imagining him with a svelte blonde or a curvy brunette and not liking the picture.

"Occasionally."

Annoyed at herself for being jealous, she gestured

toward the tennis courts and asked, "Do you play tennis when you're here?"

"Sometimes, but I'm a lousy player, and usually I've been here for medical meetings. This place has great conference facilities."

"Oh." He still could have been here with a woman. She'd seen plenty of attractive female physicians…and they'd have so much in common with Kent. She told herself she was thinking like a silly adolescent. After all, *she* was with him now.

"Can we go fishing this afternoon?" Nick asked.

"Sure," Kent answered. He grinned at Mallory. "How about you, Mom? Are you a fisherperson?"

"No way. I'm going to sit on the porch and read. You two guys enjoy yourselves."

"Okay. Nick, we have to find a shady spot. Too much sun isn't good for you."

"Okay."

Mallory marveled at her son's quick acceptance of Kent's decree. If *she'd* said the same thing, he'd at least have given her a token argument before giving in.

She watched the two of them stride off together. So much alike, from the way they held their heads to the easy, confident way they walked.

"Oh, Dean," she murmured. "What did I do to us?" Whatever she'd done, there was no undoing it. And she'd have to play this summer out the way she'd begun it. She was too afraid of what would happen if she changed course now.

She sat on the porch with a bestselling paperback on her lap but couldn't get interested in it. Instead, the afternoon sun lulled her into drowsiness. The breeze from the lake ruffled the pages of her book, and she laid it on the table beside her and shut her eyes. The drone of a motorboat broke the stillness and jarred her awake. She reached for her book again but didn't open it.

Too lazy to get up, she stayed where she was and gazed into the distance until she spied Nick and Kent coming toward her.

"Mom, guess what," Nick cried as he skipped up the porch steps.

"You caught a fish."

"Nope, we didn't catch a fish. But we saw a big turtle."

She smiled. "So the afternoon wasn't a total loss. Go get washed up. It's nearly time for dinner." She glanced at Kent. "You, too, doc."

Thirty minutes later they were seated in the airy restaurant, enjoying their meals. Afterward they headed for the twin theaters, one for children showing a recent Disney movie and the other for adults. The kids' auditorium wasn't crowded, but Kent insisted Nick sit in an isolated spot and wear a mask, just to be safe.

After getting Nick settled, Kent and Mallory headed for the grown-ups' movie, a thriller with Nicolas Cage. They found seats in the back row. The room darkened, and Kent's arm slipped around Mallory's shoulder. His finger traced circles along her upper arm, causing her skin to tingle and her heart to race as it always did when he was close.

Fifteen minutes into the movie, Mallory whispered, "I've seen this before."

Kent's breath tickled her cheek. "Wanna sneak out?"

"Sure." They got up, edged past an elderly couple and slipped out the back door of the auditorium.

Kent glanced at his watch as they crossed the lobby. "We've got a little over an hour until the kids' flick is over. Time to make it to the cabin and…"

"And?" she teased.

"Wait and see."

"We need to tell Nick we're leaving." Mallory tiptoed inside the children's theater and whispered to Nick that they'd be back soon and that he shouldn't leave the building without them.

When she returned to the lobby, Kent grabbed her hand and urged her outside. "Hurry."

Laughing like teenagers, they raced down the path toward their cabins. Mallory felt the same giddy pleasure she had years ago whenever she'd defied the no-fraternizing-with-guests rule at Comanche Trails Resort and sneaked off after work to meet Kent. If a tiny voice in her head whispered, *And where did that get you?* she ignored it.

Halfway to the cabin, she slowed, then halted, out of breath. She braced one hand against a tree trunk. "Slow down," she panted. "I'm not nineteen anymore."

Kent chuckled and hemmed her in with both hands against the tree. "Mmm, I like you better mature."

"Old?"

"Hardly." He trailed kisses across her forehead and cheeks. She shut her eyes and savored the teasing touch of his mouth, the warmth of his breath, the pleasure-pain as he nipped her lower lip. She leaned closer, and he ran his hands along her back, pulling her nearer still, letting her feel his need. "Come on," he murmured against her mouth, "or I won't be able to stop."

Neither would she, Mallory thought dizzily as he

pulled her with him down the path. At his cabin he reached in his pocket, groaning with frustration as he fumbled for his key and shoved the door open.

"Now," he muttered. "Here."

No finesse tonight. Only speed, only the fierce desire that had been building for days. They shed their clothes, tossing them away like exuberant children, laughing at each other's clumsiness. In seconds they were both naked, and Kent lowered her to the couch.

The first time he'd made love to her—the first time *any man* had made love to her—they'd been at Comanche Trails in a cabin like this. She shut her eyes and remembered, then opened them. *Don't think of then. This is now.*

Kent paused to fit on a condom, then filled her. She moaned softly with pleasure, then held him tightly as they moved together, as he fulfilled all the dreams she'd hidden in her secret heart for so many years. And when they crested and she heard him call her name, she knew beyond a doubt that the old love had never died, would live on, no matter what happened between them in the future.

They lay silently, sated. Lost in her own thoughts, Mallory stroked Kent's back. Yes, she loved him. Yes, they'd started over, but the slate wasn't clean.

"You're far away," Kent said softly. "Come back to me."

She kissed his cheek. "I'm here."

He chuckled. "Here and available?"

"So soon?" she teased.

He nipped her chin. "Try me and see."

She slipped her hand between them to stroke him. Instantly, he hardened. "Mmm, you do recover quickly," she murmured and guided him inside her.

* * *

On Sunday they drove back to Houston, detouring through Austin so Nick could see the capitol building and the famous University of Texas Tower. Despite the many new high-rise buildings in the city, these two structures dominated the skyline and defined Austin in the minds of most Texans.

"Maybe I'll go to college here," Nick said when they drove past the campus. "I'd like to be a doctor someday. Did you always know you wanted to be one, Dr. Berger?"

"Since I was your age."

"Really?"

Mallory saw the hero worship in his eyes. She whispered a silent prayer that he'd get his wish to grow up and be a doctor. Just to have him grow up strong and healthy would be enough for her.

South of the campus Kent slowed. "There's the Littlefield Fountain. Want to get out and see it and get a better look at the tower?" He found a parking space and they got out and stood for an unobstructed view of the building that symbolized the university.

Nick gawked at the fountain and its magnificent bronze sculpture. He pointed to the figure at the back. "Who's the dude with wings?"

Kent chuckled. "The dude is a lady, the goddess Columbia."

Nick shrugged. "Looks like a guy, but the tower is awesome."

Mallory smiled at the two of them and took a deep breath. She was surprised that the air had grown a bit cooler since they'd left Cedar Shores. Only the merest hint of fall wafted through the air, but it was enough to remind her that Rosh Hashanah, the Jewish New Year, and Yom Kippur, the Day of Atonement, were almost upon them. Set by a lunar calendar, their dates varied, but this year they fell in early September. "The High Holidays are in a couple of weeks," she said, over a lump in her throat.

"You're homesick," Kent said.

He always seemed to pick up on her feelings. "A little," she admitted.

He put his hand on her shoulder. "More than a little. Nick's doing well. Why don't you go home for a while?"

Home. How wonderful it would be to share the holiest days of the year with her parents. The occupants of the apartment here had become a "family," but nothing could take the place of her father's voice leading the familiar prayers, her mother's bustling in the kitchen preparing the holiday meal, the tingle of excitement at the start of a new year, a fresh start.

"But the transplant," she said. "It's been a month since the search. What if they find a donor?" She refused to add, *Or what if they don't?*

"We'll call you when we hear. Besides, the transplant doesn't happen overnight. Any possible donor would have to go through further testing."

"You're right, of course." She glanced at Nick, who had wandered off a little way. "Nicky, how would you like to go home for Rosh Hashanah?"

"Um, I guess."

Mallory frowned, then realized this trip wouldn't be easy for Nick. He wouldn't be coming home from a vacation, with stories of adventures to share with his pals. *His* adventure was like nothing they would understand. But he'd have to face that test sometime. Why not now, with the loving support of his grandparents added to hers? "I'll call the airline tomorrow."

Two nights before she left for home, Mallory lay awake. Staring out the open curtains at the night sky, she wondered how she had let herself get so involved with Kent. Answer: it was easy. She'd seen him and instantly known that the old attraction had never died. But she'd gone much further than "attraction." She'd fallen in love with Kent all over again.

She turned on her side and pulled the sheet over her shoulder. This love between them couldn't work, couldn't last. But what to do? Breaking off with Kent all of a sudden wouldn't be a good idea. That would be a blow for Nick. But she could slow things down. And now, when she was leaving for a while, was the time to do that, even though it would hurt. She'd call Kent tomorrow.

The next evening, before she had a chance to dial his number, Kent called her. "Ready to leave?" he asked.

Hearing the deep, caressing sound of his voice almost made her change her decision of last night. *No!* She steeled herself. "I'm almost packed…."

"I'll miss you."

Her heart stuttered. "I'll miss you, too."

"Thank God for Alexander Graham Bell."

Now. "I wanted to talk to you about that," she said carefully. "I don't think we should call each other while I'm gone."

Kent was silent for a moment. Then, his voice a few degrees cooler, he said, "Why's that?"

Mallory bit her lip. She was glad they weren't

face-to-face. Glad he couldn't see her wavering. "It's not that I don't want to talk to you, it's just that we've been moving so fast…"

"Maybe you're right." There was silence, then he said, "I won't argue with you. We won't talk until you're back."

"Okay." They spoke for a few moments about what time he'd pick her and Nick up to go to the airport, then hung up.

Mallory stared at the receiver in her hand. Well, she thought perversely, he'd been easy to convince. Almost too easy.

The following day Kent watched the jet lift into the air. Nick and Mallory would be gone for two weeks. Fourteen days, he told himself, to see if he could live without her, without seeing her smile, touching her hand. Without Nick, too, this youngster who had become far more important to him than a patient.

He turned away from the window. Mallory's suggestion had been unwelcome but reasonable. These two weeks apart would be a good test.

Chapter Twenty

The plane touched down at the Dallas/Fort Worth airport. Valerosa, eighty miles west of Fort Worth, was too small to have an airport of its own so anyone going there flew to DFW.

Mallory turned to Nick, whose nose was pressed against the window. "We're here." Seeing his hands moving toward his waist, she added, "Keep that seat belt on until the sign goes off."

She could hardly fault him for his excitement though. She felt the same.

After deplaning, they made their way to baggage claim. "Go sit over there, Nick," Mallory said, pointing to a chair outside the baggage area. The idea of having him in a crowded place still made her nervous.

She waited impatiently for their bags, grabbed them

off the carousel and, with Nick scurrying ahead, made her way outside.

She heard a honk, and there was her mother's car. Oblivious to the scowl of the security guard, Lydia Roseman jumped out to envelop Nick and then Mallory in her arms.

Home! Mallory felt her mother's tears on her shoulder as they hugged tight.

Behind her, Nick scrambled into the car, and Mallory heard a voice saying, "There you are at last." She turned to see Annette Brenner, Dean's mother, hugging Nick. Embracing *Kent's* son.

For the first time since the early days of her marriage to Dean, Mallory felt ill at ease seeing her mother-in-law. Dean had never told his parents that Nick wasn't his son, and now as she leaned into the car to kiss Annette, Mallory wondered if guilt was written on her face. If so, Annette didn't seem to notice. Her eyes flew back to Nick.

"Hi, Grandma Grape," he said. He'd called Annette that when he was little because she always remembered he loved grapes and had a bowl of them waiting whenever he came to her house. Mallory's mother had been Grandma Challah for the Sabbath bread she baked, but he hadn't used either term in years.

"Nick," Annette said, "you look great. I could swear you've grown another foot."

"Yep, now I have three of them."

"I see Houston hasn't changed your sense of humor, Nick," Mallory's mother said. But Mallory heard her unspoken message: *Cancer hasn't changed you.*

"Where's Dad?" Mallory asked.

"Polishing his sermons for Rosh Hashanah. You know your father." She smiled fondly. "He accepts everyone's imperfections but his own." She pulled out of the airport and onto the freeway going west. "I aired out your house, but why don't you stay with us? You won't have to cook."

"The magic words." Mallory chuckled. "I accept."

They talked nonstop all the way to Valerosa, catching up on Nick's treatment, hometown news and the burgeoning Cells Equal Life Saving.

When they drove into Valerosa, Mallory's breath caught. How wonderful to be here, to see the familiar buildings—Martin's Pharmacy, the high school, the Valerosa *Weekly Standard* building. There were the stately old trees planted along Market Street, the fountain across from city hall with its monument to the men who'd died in World War II, the playground at Oliver Park. How strange though to see that nothing had changed in Valerosa when everything had changed for her and Nick.

They pulled into her parents' driveway, and Annette walked across the street to the comfortable brick two-story house where Dean had grown up, where Mallory and Dean had shared after-school treats, where they'd practiced standing on their heads and doing long jumps, where they'd worked algebra problems together.

The Rosemans' own home, a one-story contemporary shaded by elm trees, beckoned. Nick raced inside ahead of Mallory and her mother. "Grampy," he shouted, again reverting to the name he'd used as a preschooler.

Rabbi Roseman, still walking slowly as a result of his knee surgery, came out of his study. He gave Nick a high five. "How's my superhero grandson?"

"Great. Wait till you see my signed ball from the Astros game. Clay Parker, Grampy. Can you believe it?"

"Not in a million years." Her father put his arms around Mallory, his eyes suspiciously bright.

"He's still in remission," she whispered.

"God be thanked. And may the Almighty keep him that way."

Over dinner Nick chattered about new friends, his poker-playing success and, of course, the Astros game. "Dr. Berger got us the tickets. Box seats. And he fixed it so I could meet Clay Parker." Finally he got around to talking about his treatments. "I'm being brave. Dr. Berger says I'm doing real well."

"We knew you would," his grandmother said. "But if you need some hugs or hand-holding sometimes, that's all right, too."

"I know. Can I have Brett and Steven come over tomorrow? I wanna show them my ball and teach them how to play Texas Hold 'Em."

"After they get home from school," Lydia Roseman said. "And don't forget, Rosh Hashanah begins Tuesday evening. Two more days."

That meant cleaning, cooking, polishing the silver candlesticks and wine goblet. As long as she wasn't in charge of the cooking, Mallory enjoyed getting ready almost as much as she loved the holiday itself.

On Tuesday morning, she and her mother stood at the kitchen counter. Her mother had baked a noodle kugel, a pudding made of broad noodles, apples, raisins and cinnamon. Now the smell of cinnamon permeated the room. Mallory's mouth watered. Kugel was one of her favorite holiday dishes.

She took a deep breath. Another part of home she'd missed: being in her mother's kitchen, working alongside her, listening to Lydia humming softly while she prepared the New Year's meal. "We'll have baked apples with honey this year since Nick can't eat fresh fruit," Lydia remarked. Apples with honey, the traditional Rosh Hashanah dish, represented a wish for a sweet year to come.

"I'll peel the apples after I finish getting the dressing ready," Mallory said.

Mallory enjoyed being the *assistant* to the cook; that was a job she could relate to. She crumbled bread for her mother to use in the dressing for the turkey. No matter how many times she'd tried to make the recipe herself, she always failed. She'd decided long ago that her mother had a cooking gene *she* hadn't inherited.

Lydia placed the turkey in the roaster. "Nick seems to be handling his illness very well."

"It helps that there are so many other kids around with the same disease." Mallory cracked two eggs into a bowl and began mixing them with the bread. "Our apartment is sort of like Leukemia Camp."

Her mother glanced at her. "From what Nick says, you seem to be seeing a lot of Kent Berger."

Mallory had been expecting that comment, and she knew the casual tone her mother adopted was a cover for concern. She shrugged. "We're old friends."

"And he's Nick's doctor. Is a personal relationship wise?"

Mallory's hands stilled. "Probably not. I've suggested to him that we back off for a while."

Her mother nodded. "I always liked Kent. Has he changed much?"

"Hardly at all." Enough talk about Kent, she decided. "I went by Buds and Blossoms yesterday. Lauri and I had lunch and talked about hiring someone to take my place now that summer's over and the college kids aren't around."

"Sounds like a good idea."

"Lauri's been wonderful, stepping in while Nick's been sick, but she can't handle the business alone."

While they continued talking, her mother added spices to the dressing, then stuffed the turkey and put it in the oven. Only a few more hours until the New Year began. The old year had been a rough one but hopefully this year would be better.

In the afternoon Mallory helped her mother set the table, then went to take a shower. As she passed by Nick's room, she called, "Time to get ready."

A muttered, "Yeah," mingled with the rat-a-tat-tat of an air force video game.

But when Mallory came to check on him thirty minutes later, she found Nick seated on the side of the bed, still in jeans, still absorbed in his game. "Nick, didn't you hear me tell you to get ready?"

He kept playing. "I'm not going to temple."

"Nick." When he didn't respond, she ordered, "Nick, look at me."

He shook his head, then, tears clogging his voice, said, "I don't wanna go to stupid services."

"Nick!" She'd never heard him like this. He usually loved going to temple. "What's wrong?"

"Everybody there's gonna stare at me." He ran grimy fingers over his head, where the hair was beginning to sprout, baby-fine and a lighter brown than before.

Mallory's heart shattered. She put her hand on his shoulder, felt his muscles tense. "Nicky, listen…"

"I'm not going."

"Wait." She hurried into the dining room, opened the buffet and grabbed a black skullcap. She returned to Nick's room and handed it to him. "When you wear your *yarmulke*, no one will see your hair."

He dropped the skullcap on the floor. "This stuff on my head isn't hair, it's straw."

Wishing for Kent to tell her what to do, what to say, she said, "It's your badge of honor. It shows how brave you've been."

He turned to her, his cheeks wet. "Why'd this happen to me?"

"Oh, honey," she sighed, pulling him into her arms, "I don't know. Even Grandpa doesn't know. It just did."

Nick sniffled against her shoulder. "I hate it."

"Me, too, but all both of us can do is fight it." She held him away from her. "If you really don't want to go, then don't. We'll explain to Grandma and Grandpa and we'll both stay home. We'll have our own service."

"Will Grandpa be mad?"

"He may be disappointed but he won't be mad."

Nick stared at the floor, then bent down and retrieved the skullcap. He twisted around in his hand. "I'll go," he said finally and looked up at Mallory. "Don't tell Grandpa I cried, okay?"

"Okay."

The temple was filled, the air of expectancy that always accompanied the New Year was high. This night was the threshold of the future.

Mallory, her mother and Nick made their way down the aisle to seats near the front, stopping on the way to greet friends and wish them "Happy New Year." Mallory bent to kiss Annette and Stu Brenner.

The organist entered and took his place, and the choir filed in after him. Music filled the sanctuary.

On the pulpit, Rabbi Roseman, clad in a long white robe, walked to the microphone, greeted the congregation and began the service. When they reached the Shehecheyanu, the traditional holiday prayer of thanks, he said, "This year the prayer has a special meaning to our family. We say it with joy that God has brought our grandson back to health. Please join me."

Mallory reached to one side for her mother's hand and the other for Nick's as they chanted, "Blessed art Thou, oh Lord our God, King of the Universe, who has kept us in life and sustained us and enabled us to reach this season."

Later that night as she lay in bed and relived the joy and pain of the day, Mallory wished she could share the New Year with Kent. If they were together in Houston, she'd lay her head on his shoulder, his arm would encircle her and his deep voice would vibrate in her ears. God, she missed him. She was sorry she'd placed the restriction on their talking to one another, but she wouldn't break it. "Happy New Year, Kent," she whispered and wondered what the coming months would bring for them.

In Houston several nights later Kent listened to the speaker at the fall dinner meeting of the Harris County Medical Society and hid a yawn behind his hand.

Graham Carlyle was well-respected, well-spoken…but Kent had heard much of what he was saying before. He glanced surreptitiously at his watch. Fifteen more minutes of listening to the speech, maybe twenty more schmoozing with colleagues, and then he could get the heck out of here.

Cynthia Winters, a pediatric cardiologist who was seated next to him, leaned toward him. Her eyes crinkled as she whispered, "Don't be so obvious, Doctor Berger. The speech will end. They always do."

Kent grinned. "Caught."

She yawned daintily. "We could always slip out to the bar."

Why not? Cynthia was the kind of woman he'd been drawn to since his divorce: elegant, witty and, from what he'd heard, not at all averse to a no-strings affair. But he shook his head and murmured, "Don't want to insult Carlyle. He's a good guy, even though he's a lousy speaker."

But that wasn't the only reason he said no. Cynthia had a major flaw; she wasn't Mallory, and no one else seemed to spark his interest. He was hooked.

After dinner he spent the requisite time socializing, then left. At home he stripped down to his briefs. He grabbed a beer from the fridge and wandered into his study, dropped into his armchair and reached for the phone.

He had the receiver halfway to his ear before he set it back in place. No, he wouldn't break down and call her, even though he missed her, even though he was starving for the sound of her voice.

She said they were moving too fast. Not fast *enough,*

he thought. This separation had taught him what he needed to know. He wanted her here in his home, in his life.

And Nick, too. This boy was the son he'd always wished he had. He smiled, thinking of Nick's vow to become a doctor, his delight in their fishing at Lake Travis, and his wide-eyed excitement upon meeting Clay Parker.

Parker. He'd never gotten around to printing out the pictures he'd taken at the baseball game. He'd do that now. Staying busy would lower his frustration level, and besides he'd promised Nick he'd get those pictures to him.

The photos were already on the computer. All he needed to do was enlarge them and print them out.

He found the right file: Astros. Twenty-five pictures of a memorable night from start to finish. There was the entrance to Minute Maid Park. He enlarged it and printed it out. There were Nick and Mallory posing on one of the giant baseballs. Another print.

He continued through the evening, stopping to enjoy each snapshot after he printed it. Here was a good one: Nick dumbstruck, shaking hands with Clay Parker. That was a keeper. Mallory would love it, and her parents would, too. He printed several extras.

Now the final picture, the three of them with Parker. Mallory on the pitcher's left, he and Nick on the right, all of them grinning like fools. He enlarged the photograph, waited for it to print, then picked it up for a closer look. Another keeper.

He started to lay the picture down, then stopped, looked again and frowned. He'd never noticed before, but here, standing together, smiling identical smiles, he and Nick looked enough alike to be father…and…son.

His body went rigid. Scenes played out in his mind.

The woman at McDonald's. *Your son has such nice manners. Your…son.*

His conversation with Mallory after they'd made love.

Why did you marry Dean so fast, Mallory?

Because I thought you weren't coming back.

No, because you were pregnant.

He grabbed his car keys, took the picture with him and left his house. It was after midnight, but he didn't care. He broke the speed limit getting to his office, roared into the parking lot and strode into the building.

Yanking a file drawer open, he found Nick's medical folder and took it out. Birthdate: May 17. The date of birth was just on the cusp—late if Nick were Kent's son, early if he were Dean's. Why had he never noticed the date before?

He looked again at the photo. No, not Dean's son. His. His hand closed into a fist.

Chapter Twenty-One

As the days passed, Mallory felt the peace of the holiday season envelop her like a soft blanket. Here in Valerosa, far from needles and blood count numbers, she felt her tension drain away.

Being with her parents helped. They'd always made her feel safe. Especially her mother. When Mallory had been very small and had seen her father standing on the pulpit, his deep voice resounding through the sanctuary, he'd seemed larger than life and she'd thought he might actually be God. That always made her a bit fearful. But her mom was just herself. One of Mallory's favorite of her father's proverbs was, "God could not be everywhere and so he made mothers."

Growing up in the house of a rabbi had always made

the holiday season special, and tonight was the holiest day of the Jewish year. Yom Kippur, the Day of Atonement, would begin at sunset with the Kol Nidre service in which the congregation would ask forgiveness for their sins and begin a twenty-four-hour fast. In Jewish tradition, on Rosh Hashanah God judged every human being and wrote their names in the Book of Life or the Book of Death. On Yom Kippur the decree was sealed, "Who shall live and who shall die, who shall have rest and who shall go wandering…" Mallory prayed with all her heart that Nick's name would be inscribed for life.

In the past, like a typical child, Nick had rarely thought about the meaning of Yom Kippur. It was both a day to be excused from classes and schoolwork and a time to fidget and yawn through the long services. But no longer was Nick an ordinary child. This year after the evening service Mallory heard him discussing the meaning of the holiday with his grandfather.

"We get to be forgiven for things we've done wrong, right, Grampy?"

"But just being forgiven isn't enough, is it?" Rabbi Roseman said.

"I know. We should try and do better next year."

"Good thinking." Mallory heard the pride in her father's voice. He *should* be proud. Nick was a good kid, and he understood the beauty and value of life far better than most youngsters his age.

And so did she.

As usual, the day of Yom Kippur seemed endless. Fasting was supposed to keep one's mind off worldly things, but by afternoon Mallory found it hard to concentrate on much besides her empty stomach, which growled so loudly she was sure people sitting nearby could hear it.

Her eyes went to her father on the pulpit. Watching and listening to him had always been her inspiration during the last, long hours of the fast. His stance was as tall, his voice as strong as they'd been this morning. If anything, he seemed to exude more energy than earlier in the day.

When the holiday was over, they broke their fast at the Brenners' home. The two families alternated years having a dinner and open house for friends and neighbors, and this was her in-laws' turn.

Again, Mallory felt ill at ease, especially when the Brenners focused on Nick, the grandson-who-was-not-their-grandson. At least Nick didn't chatter about Dr. Berger as he had with Mallory's parents.

She missed Kent. She knew he was leaving in the morning for a conference in Cincinnati and wouldn't be back until Monday night. She wouldn't see him until Tuesday. Four more days. Ninety-six more hours.

Her partner, Lauri, came up beside her. "Mallory, you look like you're in another world."

"I was thinking about how much has happened since last Yom Kippur."

Beth Cohen, another friend, joined them. "Nick seems to be doing well."

"Yes, thank God." Mallory glanced across the room where he sat with his plate on his lap. He'd exchanged the black skullcap he'd worn to services for his Astros cap. He and Beth's son were poking each other and laughing. He didn't look like a sick kid; he looked like any other ten-year-old.

"Are you home to stay now?" Beth asked.

"Just for the holidays. If a match turns up and Nick has his transplant, he'll have to be at the clinic for checkups every day for a hundred days."

"That's a long time in Houston," Beth said.

"Yes." But Kent was there, so to Mallory it wouldn't seem long enough.

The next morning Mallory and her mother sat in the breakfast room, sipping cups of after-breakfast coffee. They'd divided sections of the *Dallas Morning News* between them and were reading quietly when the telephone rang. "I'll get it," Mallory said and went into the kitchen. "Hello."

"Mrs. Brenner?"

"Yes."

"This is Catherine Garland."

The nurse paused, and Mallory sat down. She was certain from Catherine's tone that this wasn't good news. To postpone it, she resorted to politeness. "How are you?"

"I'm fine." The nurse paused again. "We've gotten results back from the international registry."

"And?"

"And I'm afraid we don't have a match for Nicholas."

Even sitting, Mallory felt dizzy. Her lips went numb, her vocal cords seemed paralyzed, but she forced herself to speak. "Wh-what's the next step?"

"Dr. Berger's out of town. I'll set up a time for you to talk with him about that as soon as he's back. Would Tuesday morning at nine work for you?"

"Yes, fine."

"I'm sorry the news wasn't better. Are you all right?"

"I'm okay." Carefully, Mallory set the phone down. She wasn't okay. What would they do now? Had Nick been sealed in the Book of Death?

That thought made her tears flow. She didn't even try to check them as she walked back to the breakfast room on wobbly legs.

Her mother glanced up from the newspaper. "Who— Honey, what's wrong?" She tossed the paper aside and jumped up.

Mallory almost fell into her arms. "It was about… the…the registry." Her mother's arms tightened around her. "There's…no match for Nick." Mallory sobbed harder. "What are we going to do?"

"Come, sit down." Gently her mother led Mallory back to her chair and pulled a napkin from the holder. "Dry your eyes."

Mallory sniffled. "Can't."

Her mother patted her shoulder. "Dry them before Nick hears you crying."

At that Mallory sat up and accepted the napkin from her mother's hand. She blew her nose.

"I'll bring you some water," her mother said. "Then we'll talk about what to do."

Tears threatened again. "There's nothing."

"There's always something you can do," her mother said firmly and went into the kitchen. She returned in a moment with a glass of ice water. She handed it to Mallory and sat down across from her.

Mallory sipped the water slowly, then set the half-empty glass aside. "I was so sure they'd find a match for Nick. The registry is so large." She twisted her fingers. "Maybe I should ask them to try again."

Lydia Roseman shook her head. "You'll have to talk to Nick's father."

"F-father?" Mallory stared at her mother. "But Dean's dead."

"His real father, dear. Kent Berger."

Mallory gasped. "Ke— You know?"

"I've always known," her mother said calmly. "I *can* count. And I may be a rabbi's wife, my dear, but I do know about passion."

Stunned, Mallory looked into her mother's eyes. "You never said."

"It wasn't up to me. If you'd wanted me to know, you'd have told me. If not…" She spread her hands, then grasped Mallory's. "I always knew you were in love with Kent."

"I thought if I told you, you'd be angry at me."

"I wouldn't have been angry." Her mother rubbed Mallory's cold hands. "I was disappointed that you didn't choose to confide in me, but I understood."

"Oh my God, I wish I had." Then another thought struck her. "Does Dad…?"

"Your father and I don't keep secrets from each other."

"All these years." Tears threatened again, and Mallory took a shaky breath. "I didn't want to hurt you and Dad, or embarrass you."

Her mother patted her hand. "We'd have dealt with it. But there's no use talking about it now. You and Dean were happy together."

"Yes. He saved my life."

"He knew the baby was Kent's, of course."

Mallory nodded. She told her mother the story of what she'd thought was Kent's betrayal and Dean's offer of marriage.

"And it never made a difference to him that Nick was Kent's child. He was a wonderful father."

"I know you made him happy," Lydia said. "I could see it in his eyes." She got up to clear the coffee cups and take them into the kitchen. Mallory heard the dishwasher open and close, and then her mother returned and took her place at the table. "Does Kent know about Nick?"

Mallory dropped her gaze. She shook her head.

"You have to tell him."

Mallory raised her eyes to her mother's. She knew her face was stark with pain. "He's such a wonderful doctor. I didn't want someone else to take care of Nick. I was going to wait until Nick was well."

"But now you can't." Lydia sighed. "Mallory, you know in the Kol Nidre prayer we ask God to forgive us for our sins, but those are limited to sins against God. If we've sinned against another human being, we must ask that person's forgiveness."

"Is it a sin to put your child above everyone else? I was afraid if Kent knew about Nick, he wouldn't treat his...his own son."

"I know you had the best of intentions, but that doesn't change the fact that you withheld knowledge from Kent that he'd fathered Nick."

Mallory stared at her hands. "I suppose Dad would say it's a sin of omission."

"I suppose he would."

"Kent asked me why I married Dean so quickly. I told him part of the truth. I said it was because I didn't think he was coming back."

Her mother sighed. "'Half a truth is a whole lie.' Something else your father would say."

Mallory looked up with a ghost of a smile. "I should talk to Dad tonight."

"Yes, you should. And Kent? When will you tell him about Nick?"

"He's at a conference in Cincinnati now. I'll talk to him as soon as he's back."

"You may pay a high price, but you have to tell him the truth."

Mallory repeated her mother's words to herself as she sat in the waiting room of Kent's office the following Tuesday morning. She'd set Nick's appointment for blood work at the same time as hers with Kent.

Now she watched her son flipping through a copy of *Ranger Rick* magazine. Not only would her life change this morning, but so would his. And Kent's. She should try to enjoy these last few moments. Nothing would be the same again.

But she couldn't enjoy them. Sitting on the edge of her chair, she clasped her hands tightly in her lap. In one brief moment years ago, she'd strayed too far from the straight path and veered into a labyrinth. And now she couldn't get out.

She and Kent had been young, carefree and in love the night they had gone to Bear Creek Park. They'd spread a blanket on the bank and lain side by side, then Kent had said lazily, "Want to go swimming?"

"Sure." Mallory pulled off her T-shirt to reveal a bikini top. She smiled at the way Kent's eyes darkened when she rose and slipped out of her shorts. Feminine power sparked through her.

"Race you to the water," she said saucily and took

off without looking back, knowing she had the advantage because he was still dressed. She was a strong swimmer; she'd been on the swim team from junior high on. She was two lengths away from the shore when he grabbed her ankle.

"Darn, you're quick," she said, flailing in her effort to get away. He held on and pulled her back to him. She waited until he let her go, then cupped her hands and flung them up out of the water, splashing him full in the face. He ducked her and she came up sputtering and splashed him again.

Laughing and shrieking like children, they continued their water fight until Mallory shouted, "Enough!"

"Say uncle."

"Never." She flipped over, intending to streak away, but he caught her again.

"Come here," he ordered and dragged her into his arms for a quick, hard kiss. "Oh, no," he said, grabbing the hand she was moving furtively toward the water. "No more splashing." He held her in place while he surveyed her with a lazy smile. "I bet you've never been skinny-dipping."

"No-o, but—" She twisted one arm free and unfastened the top of her swimsuit. With the swatch of cloth hanging from one finger, she gave him an arch smile.

His eyes almost black now, Kent bent to suckle one distended nipple, then the other. His hold on her tightened, his breathing deepened. "God, Mallory," he groaned, "I've got to have you. Now."

"Yes, now." As ravenous as he, she let go of him to struggle with the bottom of her suit. Yanking at the cloth, she forgot to tread water and sank into a dim, translucent world. Kent was a shadow beside her, dragging his trunks down over his hips. Freed from clothing, they broke the surface and tossed their suits onto the bank.

The water, so icy before, seemed to sizzle. Never thinking of protection, mad to hold, to possess, they came together with raw, mindless need.

Later she lay on the blanket, curled against Kent. The breeze whispered over her skin. The night was quiet save for the singing of crickets in the trees and the soft lapping of water against the shore.

Awed by the intensity of their lovemaking, Mallory gazed up at the moon. Not quite full now, it seemed like a golden eye, winking down at them knowingly, not at all surprised by their frenzied coupling.

Had their wild lovemaking in the water been some kind of moon madness? Midsummer lust? She didn't know for certain. She only knew that it was something different, something…extraordinary.

And now she would pay the price.

"Mrs. Brenner." Catherine Garland's voice yanked her back into the present. "Doctor Berger is ready for you. Nick, this way. The vampires are ready to take your blood."

Nick grinned. "Oooh, scary."

Scary hardly described what Mallory felt as she walked slowly toward Kent's office. Her heart pounded, her pulse beat crazily. She wished this were over. She wished she was a thousand miles away.

She opened Kent's door. He was on the phone, taking notes. Barely looking up, he waved her toward a chair. She sat down. Waited.

Finally he hung up, faced her. "Good morning."

Something was different. His eyes were cool, his demeanor distant. But she didn't have time to wonder about that now. "Good morning," she murmured, then when he said nothing more, she cleared her throat. "I guess you've heard there isn't a match for Nick."

He nodded. "Catherine told me this morning."

Mallory leaned forward. "W-would you consider being tested?"

"I already have."

Thunderstruck, she stared at him. "You...you have? When?"

"Last week," he replied. "Did you think I'd let *my son* die?"

Chapter Twenty-Two

Stunned, Mallory gaped at Kent. "Y-you *know?*"

"Yes." His voice chilled her to the bone. "I admit I'm a little slow, but I finally figured it out."

"How?" she whispered.

"Picture from the baseball game." He reached in his drawer, retrieved a photograph and tossed it across the desk. "And this weekend I took a side trip from Cincinnati to New Concord to visit my folks. I found a picture of myself at Nick's age." The second photo followed the first.

Mallory stared at the pictures. Identical. But for the difference in the snapshot dates, Kent and Nick could have been twins. She looked up from the photographs and met Kent's eyes. "I…"

"When were you planning to tell me?" he asked with a grimace of disgust. "Or were you?"

"Yes, I was. Later. When Nick was well."

"When he was well for how long? A month? A year? Five years, posttransplant?"

"It's not like that." She spoke on a sob. "I wanted Nick to have the best doctor, and that was you. I needed your medical expertise."

"And now you need my bone marrow, so you moved up the confession date." He stood. "Well, you've 'confessed.' I've had the screening test and I've asked that they put a rush on it. Dr. Ratcliff will be seeing Nick from now on. Dr. McNeece in bone marrow will let you know about the test results."

Mallory rose, her voice pleading. "Oh, God, I knew this would happen if I told you. I had to put Nick's needs first. I couldn't take a chance with his life. Can't you understand? I wanted *you* as his doctor. I still do."

"Not possible. I can't treat my own son."

"That's why I didn't tell you."

He didn't answer. Instead he sat, reached for a folder on his desk, opened it and began to read.

She'd been cruelly dismissed. She guessed she deserved it.

Mallory stood still for a moment, willing Kent to look up and meet her eyes. But he didn't. Finally she turned and walked stiffly out the door, surprised she didn't stumble on the way to the waiting room.

When she got there, she saw that Nick was not back. Thank heavens. He was perceptive enough to recognize that something was wrong with her.

She sank into a chair and shut her eyes. The waiting

room was generally a friendly place, but she didn't want to talk or even look at anyone this morning.

Her thoughts spun like pinwheels, one blotting out another before it was finished. Would Kent try to take Nick away from her? Or at least sue for joint custody? How would Nick feel about suddenly having a new doctor? Would his recovery be affected?

At least she was certain of one thing: If Kent were a match, he'd donate. As he'd said, there was no way he'd let his son die. Lord, how was she going to continue bringing Nick to the clinic where she might run in to Kent? Should she transfer Nick to another hospital? But that didn't make sense at this stage of his treatment.

"Mom, you asleep?"

Mallory started at Nick's voice. She opened her eyes and straightened. "I have a headache."

"You can take medicine for it, right?"

She gathered her purse and stood. "Right, and maybe I'll lie down for a while at home."

"Do I get to see Dr. Berger this morning?" he asked as she urged him toward the door.

"No, um, I need to talk to you about that."

"Okay," he said obligingly.

"In the car."

They were silent in the elevator and as they walked across the parking lot, but as soon as Nick was seated with his belt fastened, he asked, "What's the secret?"

Mallory started the car. "There's no secret. I just don't like to discuss medical things in the elevator or the hall." She backed out of her space slowly, afraid her jumbled emotions would interfere with her driving. When she turned onto the street, she said, "Dr. Berger's pretty busy right now with...um, some research he's doing, so Dr. Ratcliff will be your doctor for...for a while." As she glanced at Nick's face, she knew she couldn't say Dr. Ratcliff would see him permanently.

Nick's expression was half-hurt, half-furious. "No way!"

"This isn't negotiable, Nick."

"Bummer." His eyes filled with tears. "I thought Dr. Berger liked me."

She handed him a tissue. "He does, sweetie, but this research is important."

"*I'm* not important?" He had such a stricken look on his face that Mallory pulled off the street and into a parking lot. She unbuckled her seat belt, leaned across the console and put her arms around Nick. "Of course you're important. But Dr. Berger's research is about something that will help thousands of kids."

What had she told herself a few weeks ago? One lie begets another. "You know, Nicky, by giving up Dr. Berger's time, you'll be contributing to his research, too, in a way, right?"

Nick didn't answer.

"Right?" Mallory cajoled.

"I guess."

She started the car again, then put her foot on the brake. "Look, there's an ice-cream shop over there. Let's treat ourselves."

"In the middle of the morning?" A sly smile appeared. "I must be really upset if you're bribing me with ice cream before lunch. Can I have two scoops?"

"One. Don't push it, kiddo," she said as she drove across the lot and parked in front of the store.

Nick ordered a scoop of his favorite: Baseball Nut. Mallory ordered chocolate mint, but even chocolate couldn't obliterate the pain she felt inside.

As soon as they got home, she reminded Nick of her "headache" and went to her room. She shut the door, got out her cell phone and dialed her parents' home.

"Shalom, this is Rabbi Roseman," her father said.

"Hi, Dad. Would you put Mom on the other phone?" Mallory struggled to keep the tears back as she told her parents what had happened.

"You did the right thing," her father said firmly. "I'm proud of you."

"Give Kent some time," her mother advised. "Maybe after he's had time to think, he'll calm down, and the two of you can talk."

"I don't know."

"You did what Nick needed, just as you've done all along," her mother said. "Keep that in the front of your mind."

"I'll try." Mallory wasn't sure Kent would ever "calm down," but talking to her parents did bolster her spirits. She hung up and took the spread off her bed. She really did have a headache.

She went into the bathroom, dampened a washcloth with cool water and laid it across her forehead. She shut her eyes, and when she opened them again and glanced at the clock, she saw that she'd slept past lunchtime. Good thing Nick had had that ice-cream cone. She went out to the kitchen and found him fixing a peanut butter and jelly sandwich.

"Want one?" he asked.

"No thanks." The thought of food made her feel sick. She wondered if she'd ever feel hungry again.

For the rest of the day Kent saw patients, made rounds and wrote orders as usual, but bitterness and anger simmered below the surface. Mallory had betrayed him again. "Fool me once, shame on you. Fool me twice, shame on me," he muttered.

How could he have been so dense? How could he not have seen what was right before his eyes? He wondered how many others had figured out that he was Nick's father. Then he decided probably no one had. People saw what they wanted to see or were conditioned to, and Mallory, damn her, had conditioned everyone quite well.

He wondered when Nick had been conceived...and then he knew. That night at the lake. They'd been crazy, impulsive, with never a thought to protection.

He'd missed ten years of his son's life. And when Mallory took Nick home to Valerosa, he'd miss even more. Not completely, he promised himself. He'd find a way to be part of Nick's life from now on.

He went into his office, removed his white lab coat and hung it up. Sitting at his desk, he checked his schedule for tomorrow.

Had Dean known who Nick's father was? Or did Mallory hoodwink him, too? "Hoodwink"—the perfect word for what she'd done.

His phone rang. He considered ignoring it, but despite his personal pain, he was a physician. He picked up the receiver. "Dr. Berger."

"Kent, it's Ray McNeece. Got a few minutes?"

"A few."

"How about meeting me for a drink?"

"Yeah." A drink sounded like a good idea. He could drown his sorrows in booze. Not the way he usually handled problems, but what the hell? "Where and what time?" he asked.

"Amelia's at six-thirty. That okay with you?"

"I'll be there."

Amelia's was a pleasant spot and only a block from Gaines Memorial. Kent decided to walk. Now that it was late September and the heat was dying down, the evening was pleasant, and besides, exercise was known to be a good remedy for whatever might ail someone.

Due to its location, Amelia's was popular with doctors and other medical professionals. It had a bar and a couple of good-sized dining rooms, all wood paneled for a cozy feel. Outside was a stone patio with colored lanterns. He'd planned to take Mallory here sometime when the weather was cooler so they could sit on the patio as they had at the Lark's Nest. Hah. That would never happen now.

His colleague from the bone marrow department wasn't there yet when he arrived. He asked for a table inside, ordered a scotch and waited, staring morosely into his glass.

"How's it going?"

Kent looked up when he heard Ray's voice. "Okay," he lied. "You?"

They made small talk for a while, then Ray said, "I have the results of your screening. Looks like you're a fifty percent match for the Brenner kid."

Kent's heart caught. A match for Nick. His fingers tightened around his glass. "That's great," he said softly.

"Of course we'll have to get another blood sample and do more extensive testing to confirm." Kent nodded, and McNeece asked, "If we do confirm, are you planning to be the boy's donor?"

"Of course."

McNeece glanced down and swirled the liquid in his glass. "Look, Kent, I don't know what the relationship is between you and the Brenner boy." He held up a hand as Kent started to answer. "I'm not fishing. I was going to add that I don't want to know. But you have to realize that even though we'll be as discreet as possible, your being this youngster's donor is going to set a lot of tongues wagging. You'll have to be prepared to deal with that."

"I've already given some thought to the possible… repercussions." Kent took a sip of scotch. "I'll deal with them. The only thing that really matters is that Nick have a chance at life."

The following week Mallory got a phone call from Dr. McNeece's nurse, asking her to come in for a conference. Again she set the appointment during Nick's visit to the leukemia clinic.

She knew this had to be about Kent's blood test. There was no one else who'd been screened.

When they arrived at the clinic and she took her keys from the ignition, she saw that her hand was shaking. She willed it to stop. She couldn't be so anxious in front of Nick.

She dropped him off and headed upstairs to the bone marrow clinic. She sat in the waiting room and tried to be calm, but her stomach was turning flip-flops. Good thing she had skipped breakfast because she was certain she couldn't keep it down.

"Mrs. Brenner."

She jumped at her name, sprang up and hurried through the door. She felt as if she'd been on trial and was about to hear the verdict. Would this be a chance for Nick or not?

When she entered his office, Dr. McNeece stood and said a brisk, "Good morning." She tried to read his eyes to see if the news was good or bad but couldn't. She sat down and waited.

"I have two pieces of news for you," he said, then broke into a smile. "Both good."

She let out the breath she'd been holding. "Yes?"

"First of all, the blood screening test from the… potential donor showed a fifty percent match."

"Oh, my God," Mallory whispered. "That's wonderful."

"We got the second blood sample and expedited the in-depth testing," the doctor continued, "and the match is still fifty percent."

"Then…then Nick can have the transplant?"

"The donor is good to go."

Mallory noticed he was careful not to reveal the donor's name. "So are we," she said. "As soon as possible."

"Don't decide yet," McNeece said.

She frowned. "I don't understand."

"You have another option, one that wasn't available even last week. Gaines Memorial got a call three days ago inviting us to participate in a clinical trial of a new drug for acute myelogenous leukemia. During the first stage of trials, the drug was extremely successful in putting patients of all ages in remission. The patients have been followed for over five years. The majority are considered cured. The stage-two trial will involve many more patients. I'm giving you the option of having Nicholas participate."

Mallory stared at the physician as she digested his words. "And doing that would mean he wouldn't need a transplant?"

"Correct."

"But what if it doesn't work?"

"We can do the transplant later." He met her eyes and smiled. "And another piece of good news. The drug is given intravenously in three doses, each a month apart. Nicholas would be hospitalized for the IV and then for two more days of observation. We'd do the first dose here and the other two could be given at your local hospital. Then we'd check him ninety days later." He smiled again. "Why don't you think it over and give me your answer Monday?"

No transplant. Home. She didn't even have to think about it. "I'll give it to you now," she said. "Yes."

Chapter Twenty-Three

Two weeks later Mallory and Nick were ready to leave for Valerosa. Mallory hefted the last suitcase into the trunk and slammed it shut. Nick was already in the car, seat belt fastened. She took one last look at the apartment building that had been their home all these months and pulled out of the parking lot and into the street.

She had a lot to be thankful for. Nick was well on the way to conquering his illness, to returning to normal life. People, older ones usually, always stressed the importance of having their health, but no one truly comprehended that unless their own health was suddenly snatched away. She understood now; so did Nick. He'd traveled through the long, dark tunnel of illness and climbed back into the sunlight. No one in their family would ever take good health for granted again.

But leaving Houston was bittersweet. Not only would she miss the medical staff at Gaines Memorial, but she and Nick had made so many friends in Houston, found such support and camaraderie. Saying goodbye to the other families had been tough. They'd all promised to keep in touch, and the CELS group, now under Karen's leadership, would remain important in all their lives. In fact, Mallory planned to fly back to Houston to meet with Veronica Mason next month to discuss Veronica's role in the organization.

Tamara had taken on the responsibility for the rose garden that Mallory had planted behind the apartment. The parents' group planned to enlarge it, to add more bushes as new patients arrived. "Someday it will get too big for the apartment. We'll have to transplant the bushes to the medical center," Tamara said. "I'm already picturing it around a new patio at Gaines Memorial."

Mallory imagined the garden there as she drove past the hospital. Then she turned the corner and a few minutes later guided the car up the ramp and onto the freeway, heading northwest.

Her heart still ached over the debacle with Kent. She knew she'd always carry that pain with her. How could she not? Every time she looked at Nick she saw Kent's face.

Yet she didn't see how she could have handled the situation any other way. Nick came first.

She'd tried to get in touch with Kent to tell him again why she hadn't been honest with him about Nick. She'd hoped she could explain it better this time so that even if he couldn't forgive her, he'd understand. She wanted to leave on at least neutral terms with him, not with anger and bitterness between them. But he hadn't returned her calls.

She tried his home but no one answered. He probably saw her name on caller ID and chose not to pick up.

Finally she left a message on his machine: "Kent, I know I've hurt you. I know you're angry. But please believe me, I never meant to cause you pain. I'm a mother and like any mother, I put my child—*our* child—first. I hope you can understand this and that someday you'll forgive me.

"I have so much to thank you for—first for giving me Nick. He's a wonderful kid, and he has so much of you in him. And second for giving Nick his life back, by your medical treatment and your offer of bone marrow. Nothing could mean more.

"We'll be leaving Houston soon. I wish I could tell you goodbye in person, but since I can't, this will have to do. I wish you well. I love you, Kent. You'll always, *always* be in my heart."

She'd never know Kent's reaction to the message. Even after she'd poured out her heart, he didn't call.

Well, she'd done all she could. She drove along in silence, then as Houston disappeared behind them, Nick said, "We should have stopped at the clinic to say goodbye to Dr. Berger."

Mallory bit her lip. *Don't give in to tears,* she told herself. "Dr. Berger's busy. He's probably in the clinic this morning, seeing patients."

"Yeah, I know. You know, Mom, I was hoping you and he would, like, get together."

She turned and stared at him. "Get together?"

"Like, get married."

"Oh, honey. Dr. Berger and I are just friends." *Were.*

"Friends get married sometimes, don't they? You and

Dad were friends." He sighed and added wistfully, "I really wished hard that you'd marry Dr. Berger. He'd be a cool dad."

"Ah…" What should she say? He *is* your dad. Sure, tell him right now in the car.

Nick didn't seem to notice her hesitation. "The other day he said I could come and visit him in Houston."

"He did?" Fear clutched at her. Did that mean Kent would try to get custody of Nick? "When did you two talk about that?" She'd tried to make her voice sound casual but it came out as a croak.

"When I had my last blood test. He always comes in to talk to me."

Surely Kent hadn't told him. "Wh-what do you talk about?" she asked.

"Oh, stuff." He grinned. "Guy stuff. Baseball, NASA, what it takes to be a doctor."

Mallory couldn't help but smile at that. "There are women doctors, too, or haven't you noticed?"

"Come on, Mom. Sure I have. But, you know, I wanted to find out how *he* got to be one."

Kent was his hero, for sure.

He's out of your life. Nick's, too. Stop thinking about him, she ordered herself and kept driving.

Once they were settled at home, Mallory kept herself busy. She made arrangements for Nick to start school, half time at first, and found a retired teacher who would tutor him several times a week to help him catch up. She set up an appointment schedule for him with Dr. Sanders. And she went back to work. She loved being in her shop, inhaling the scent of flowers, making beautiful arrangements for customers. Life went on as it always had.

At first Mallory was fearful that Kent would try to take Nick away from her. After all, he was a successful doctor with plenty of money, living in a city with far more to offer than a small town in north Texas. But as time went on and nothing happened, her fears lessened. At times she was even somewhat annoyed that Kent made no effort to keep in contact with Nick. Then, as the weeks passed, she told herself he was probably involved with another woman by now and wasn't thinking of Nick…or her…at all.

Nick came through his next two IV treatments without incident. He returned to school full-time and was already talking about playing Little League in the spring. As Thanksgiving approached and Buds and Blossoms was overwhelmed with holiday orders, Mallory thought perhaps her heartbreak over Kent was beginning to heal.

But she knew she was fooling herself. At night he invaded her dreams, making love to her so ardently that she woke trembling. In those dark hours she faced the fact that she'd never be over him.

In Houston, Kent meandered through the Galleria. Thanksgiving was over and he'd put off Chanukah shopping too long. He needed gifts for his parents, sister and brother-in-law and two nephews. Normally he didn't mind shopping, but this year he didn't have the holiday spirit. Festive decorations, eye-catching displays and the sound of carols made him feel glum. He found himself impatient with sales clerks, with jostling crowds and noisy people. He scowled at a man who bumped against him and just missed stepping on his foot. Damn, he was turning into Scrooge.

He decided to start with gifts for his nephews. They were six and nine and already techno freaks. He headed for World of Toys, passing Santa's kingdom on the way. Santa looked appropriately fat and jolly. His elves snapped pictures, herded kids back and forth. Children, some excited, some whiny, were lined up along the walkway while their parents tried to keep them from wandering off. Kent turned away from the families. *Happy families. Bah! Humbug!*

The toy store was crowded, too. He found a model of the space shuttle along with toy astronauts for Bryan, the six-year-old who loved outer space paraphernalia. Then he wandered over to the video games and picked one for Seth.

Beside him, a father and son debated the merits of two new games. "This one has better graphics," the father said.

"Yeah, but this one is mega-exciting," his son argued.

Kent glanced at the two, noticing that neither seemed to think this an extraordinary occasion. And why should they? This man had doubtless been with his son since the boy's birth. Why should a trip to the mall be anything special?

The guy didn't have any idea how special it was, Kent thought. He'd give anything to be standing here with his son, having the same discussion. God, he missed the boy.

Should he buy a Chanukah gift for Nick?

A present wasn't enough. He wanted to see Nick.

He'd thought of asking for shared custody, but he

hadn't. He couldn't get past the obstacle of telling Nick he was his father. How would the boy take it?

Useless to wonder. Mallory wouldn't let that happen.

He stood uncertainly in front of the video games display, then grabbed another of the one he'd bought for Seth. If he didn't, the stores might be out by the time he made his decision on what to do about Nick.

He paid for his purchases, arranged to have the gifts for his nephews mailed and left the mall. Chanukah was an eight-day holiday. The rest of his family would have to wait until the last day to receive their gifts.

At home, he went into his study, sat behind the desk and stared into space. How could he have Nick in his life? How could he fill the hole in his heart?

The answer was obvious. He could ask Mallory to marry him.

But marrying her for Nick wasn't enough, wasn't fair.

He opened his desk drawer and took out the answering machine tape with Mallory's message. Despite his anger at her, he hadn't been able to allow the machine to tape over her words.

He turned the tape around in his hand. He hadn't listened to it since he'd first heard it. He would now.

He took out the current tape from his machine and slipped this one in, then played it.

"Kent, I know I've hurt you…" Her voice. "…I didn't mean to cause you pain…" And finally, "…you'll always, always be in my heart."

He played the tape again.

Why hadn't he understood a mother's need to put her son's life before everything else? He'd been so angry and hurt, he hadn't even tried to understand Mallory's predicament.

He pictured Mallory standing beside him at Lake Travis, the wind blowing through her hair; remembered her face turned toward his in the hospital, her eyes full of trust; relived nights in her arms, her warm body snuggled next to his. His heart ached with longing. Not just for Nick. For her, too.

Damn, he was a fool. He did want to marry Mallory, but not only because of Nick. He was still in love with her.

But was it too late?

The next week Mallory stood in her kitchen, polishing the silver Chanukah menorah. She loved the holiday, with its message of courage, when the Jews had withstood the might of an empire to keep their religious freedom. She loved the Chanukah miracle, the light in the temple that was rekindled after the rebellion was over. With only enough oil for one day, the light had burned for eight days.

Mallory glanced at her watch and smiled to herself. Nick would be home from school soon. He—

The doorbell rang, startling her. She set the menorah on the counter and hurried into the living room. She peered through the front door peephole...and gasped.

Kent stood outside her door.

Was he here to take Nick away from her?

Hand trembling, she opened the door.

They stood staring at each other. "Mallory," he said softly.

A brisk December breeze set off a flurry of leaves. Mallory shivered. "May I come in?" Kent asked.

"Oh...sure." She stepped aside. He came in, bringing

cold air and the scent of sandalwood. To give herself a moment to settle, she said, "I'll, um, take your jacket." He shrugged out of it and she hung it in the entry closet. "Sit down."

He took a seat on the sofa and she sat in an armchair, diagonal to the couch. The best defense was a strong offense, she told herself. "Why are you here?" she asked.

"To see you."

"To see *Nick*."

He sighed. "Yes, of course." He glanced at the clock on the mantel. "I assume he's still at school."

"Yes."

"Then we have time to talk."

She regarded him warily. "About what?"

He bent his head for a moment, then looked up. "About how sorry I am for the way I acted the last time I saw you. I was angry."

"That was obvious. What you said to me hurt," she admitted, "but I guess you had a right." She gazed into his eyes. "I hurt you, too. When I got pregnant, I was young, I was scared. This summer...well, you know about that."

He leaned toward her and surprised her by saying, "I understand."

"Do you?"

"Took a while, but yes."

"Is that why you came?" she asked. "To tell me?"

"That's one reason." He paused, then said, "And to see if we can start over again."

"Meaning?"

"You left me a message." He leaned forward and grasped her hand. "You said you loved me. If you still do, or if you think you can again, will you marry me?"

She'd never imagined this would happen, but she needed more from him. "Do you want to get married so you'll have Nick?"

"Yes," he said, and her heart fell. "But more important than that, I want to get married because I love you. Only you."

At his words her breath caught. Her lips curved into a joyful smile. She didn't need time to think. "Then the answer is yes," she said. "Because I love you, too."

They both stood at the same time. He opened his arms and she went into them. At last she was truly home.

An hour later the front door opened and banged shut. "Mom," Nick called.

"In the kitchen. Come here. We have company."

"Yeah, there's a car outsi—" He stopped in the doorway. "Dr. Berger."

Kent got up from his chair and walked over to give Nick a high five. "How're you doing, pal?"

"Great. You're in a different car. Did something happen to your Jaguar?"

"It's fine. I flew to Dallas and rented a car."

Mallory smiled to herself. Trust guys to think of cars first and foremost.

Nick dumped his backpack on the floor, then looked warily at Kent. "Why are you here? My blood counts are okay, aren't they?"

Kent put his hand on Nick's shoulder. "Sure they are. This isn't a doctor visit." He glanced at Mallory, she nodded and he smiled. "I came to ask your mom a question. I asked her if she'd marry me."

Nick's eyes got huge. "Did you say yes, Mom?"

Mallory grinned. "Yes, I did."

Nick grinned back. "I wanted this so bad. I guess my wish finally came true." He glanced at the menorah sitting on the counter with the first candle in place for that evening. "It's like a Chanukah miracle."

"You're our miracle," she said and hugged both her men close to her heart.

Epilogue

Houston
Eight years later

The high school auditorium was crowded. A buzz of excitement filled the air as the graduates of Armstrong High School began walking across the stage to claim their diplomas. This was a night to celebrate. Mallory and Kent sat, hands clasped. Their two daughters, Amanda and Rence, sat on either side of them. Farther down the row Mallory's parents and Kent's sat together. Dean's folks hadn't been able to come but they'd sent their love.

"Susan Bailey," the principal announced.

"They're going across the stage in ABC order, right, Mommy?" seven-year-old Amanda whispered.

"You're right, honey."

"Then it's almost time for Nick."

Mallory nodded, her heart full. Eight years ago she'd feared this night would never come.

"Nicholas Berger."

"Yeah, Nicky," five-year-old Renee cried.

Mallory let go of Kent's hand to clap. As he crossed the stage, her heart filled with pride for Nick's achievements and she whispered a prayer of gratitude for his continued good health. He was a special young man. He'd learned from his illness to take nothing for granted. He realized he could surmount any obstacle, face any challenge. Because he'd faced the worst.

Cancer-free since his clinical trial, Nick had long ago stopped living under the shadow of disease. He'd played baseball again and caught up with his classmates in school. His goals hadn't changed; he still intended to be a doctor. Next year he'd attend Duke University.

Mallory and Kent looked at each other. There'd been plenty of roadblocks on the way to this day, but they, too, had managed to overcome them all.

They'd waited to tell Nick that Kent was his father until they were certain he was both well and mature enough to understand.

They'd been wrong. He *hadn't* understood. His first reaction was to refuse to believe what they said. Then for months he'd acted out, refused to speak to Kent, let his grades drop and made all their lives miserable. Mallory had finally insisted that all of them get counseling. And slowly Nick had come around.

One night he'd come to them and said, "Y'know, I realize I'm pretty lucky. I have two dads."

After that his relationship with Kent improved, and the two of them, so much alike, became even closer than they'd been earlier.

Mallory had not told Dean's family that Nick was Kent's son but she suspected they'd figured it out from the strong resemblance between Kent and Nick. Still, she'd remained close with them and so had Nick.

Mallory smiled as Nick walked off the stage and took his seat. She nestled her hand in Kent's once more, then turned to him and found his eyes on her.

Whatever the future held for them, they'd face it together. Her lips formed the words, "I love you."

Kent squeezed her hand and whispered back, "I love you, too. Only you."

* * * * *

New York Times *bestselling author*
Linda Lael Miller
is back with a new romance
featuring the heartwarming McKettrick family
from Silhouette Special Edition.

SIERRA'S HOMECOMING
by Linda Lael Miller

On sale December 2006,
wherever books are sold.

Turn the page for a sneak preview!

Soft, smoky music poured into the room.

The next thing she knew, Sierra was in Travis's arms, close against that chest she'd admired earlier, and they were slow dancing.

Why didn't she pull away?

"Relax," he said. His breath was warm in her hair.

She giggled, more nervous than amused. What was the matter with her? She was attracted to Travis, had been from the first, and he was clearly attracted to her. They were both adults. Why not enjoy a little slow dancing in a ranch-house kitchen?

Because slow dancing led to other things. She took a step back and felt the counter flush against her lower back. Travis naturally came with her, since they were holding hands and he had one arm around her waist.

Simple physics.

Then he kissed her.

Physics again—this time, not so simple.

"Yikes," she said, when their mouths parted.

He grinned. "Nobody's ever said that after I kissed them."

She felt the heat and substance of his body pressed against hers. "It's going to happen, isn't it?" she heard herself whisper.

"Yep," Travis answered.

"But not tonight," Sierra said on a sigh.

"Probably not," Travis agreed.

"When, then?"

He chuckled, gave her a slow, nibbling kiss. "Tomorrow morning," he said. "After you drop Liam off at school."

"Isn't that…a little…soon?"

"Not soon enough," Travis answered, his voice husky. "Not nearly soon enough."

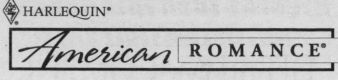

HARLEQUIN®

American ROMANCE®

IS PROUD TO PRESENT

COWBOY VET
by Pamela Britton

Jessie Monroe is the last person on earth
Rand Sheppard wants to rely on, but he needs
a veterinary technician—yesterday—and she's the
only one for hire. It turns out the woman who
destroyed his cousin's life isn't who Rand thought
she was. And now she's all he can think about!

"Pamela Britton writes the kind of
wonderfully romantic, sexy, witty romance
that readers dream of discovering
when they go into a bookstore."

—*New York Times* bestselling author
Jayne Ann Krentz

Cowboy Vet *is available from*
Harlequin American Romance in December 2006.

REQUEST YOUR FREE BOOKS!

2 FREE NOVELS PLUS 2 *FREE GIFTS!*

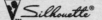

SPECIAL EDITION™

Life, Love and Family!

YES! Please send me 2 FREE Silhouette Special Edition® novels and my 2 FREE gifts. After receiving them, if I don't wish to receive any more books, I can return the shipping statement marked "cancel." If I don't cancel, I will receive 6 brand-new novels every month and be billed just $4.24 per book in the U.S., or $4.99 per book in Canada, plus 25¢ shipping and handling per book and applicable taxes, if any*. That's a savings of at least 15% off the cover price! I understand that accepting the 2 free books and gifts places me under no obligation to buy anything. I can always return a shipment and cancel at any time. Even if I never buy another book from Silhouette, the two free books and gifts are mine to keep forever.

235 SDN EEYU   335 SDN EEY6

Name _____ (PLEASE PRINT)

Address _____ Apt. _____

City _____ State/Prov. _____ Zip/Postal Code _____

Signature (if under 18, a parent or guardian must sign)

Mail to Silhouette Reader Service™:

IN U.S.A.	IN CANADA
P.O. Box 1867	P.O. Box 609
Buffalo, NY	Fort Erie, Ontario
14240-1867	L2A 5X3

Not valid to current Silhouette Special Edition subscribers.

Want to try two free books from another line?
Call 1-800-873-8635 or visit www.morefreebooks.com.

* Terms and prices subject to change without notice. NY residents add applicable sales tax. Canadian residents will be charged applicable provincial taxes and GST. This offer is limited to one order per household. All orders subject to approval. Credit or debit balances in a customer's account(s) may be offset by any other outstanding balance owed by or to the customer. Please allow 4 to 6 weeks for delivery.

SSE06

COMING NEXT MONTH

SPECIAL EDITION

#1795 SIERRA'S HOMECOMING—Linda Lael Miller
McKettrick Women
After moving to the family ranch, single mom Sierra McKettrick had enough trouble fending off handsome caretaker Travis Reid, without having to worry whether the Triple M was haunted! Yet strange events led her to discover she was living a parallel life with her ancestor, whose ethereal presence offered Sierra a lesson in hope and love.

#1796 RILEY AND HIS GIRLS—Janis Reams Hudson
Tribute, Texas
When her best friend, army sergeant Brenda Sinclair, was killed in action, Amy Galloway went to Tribute, Texas, to support the family. What Amy didn't expect was the comfort builder Riley Sinclair and his three little girls offered in return. As the Rileys drew this plain Jane out of her shell, Amy realized that Tribute was starting to feel a lot like home.

#1797 THE SUPER MOM—Karen Rose Smith
Talk of the Neighborhood
Though she was known around Danbury Way as Supermom, Angela Schumacher was at her wits' end raising three kids and working two jobs…until her son's irresistible Big Brother, high school football coach, David Moore, offered his *very* personal support. But would her ex-husband's interference cause Angela to fumble David's affections?

#1798 BABY STEPS—Karen Templeton
Babies, Inc.
Shy shop owner Dana Malone knew it was wrong to long for gorgeous Realtor C. J. Turner. But when her cousin left a baby on Dana's doorstep—and a birth certificate claiming C.J. was the father!—the unlikely couple rallied to raise the child. And C.J. found himself taking baby steps toward a real commitment to this special woman.

#1799 THE DATE NEXT DOOR—Gina Wilkins
To avoid his classmates' unwanted sympathy at his high school reunion, widowed pediatrician Joel Brannon recruited his neighbor, police officer Nicole Sawyer, as his date. Nic gamely went along with the ruse, but the "pity date" soon threatened to become the real thing.

#1800 THE MAN FROM MONTANA—Mary J. Forbes
She was a woman of words; he was a man who avoided them as much as possible. But journalist Rachel Brant needed that interview, and Ash McKee was the way she was going to get it. She was determined to get her story. Would she soon get her man, as well?

SSECNM1106